D1152549

FRIENDS AT WAR

Alan Lambert

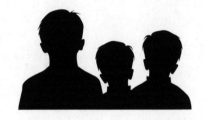

Pont

For Romy

Published in 2012 by Pont Books, an imprint of
Gomer Press, Llandysul, Ceredigion SA44 4JL

ISBN 978 1 84851 466 9

A CIP record for this title is available from the British Library.

This book is published with the financial support of the
Welsh Books Council.

Printed and bound in Wales at
Gomer Press, Llandysul, Ceredigion SA44 4JL

Chapter 1

The plane came screaming out of the sky.

'Raider overhead!' shouted Freddo. Then he fell to the ground, clutching his neck. 'Owwww!' he moaned. 'I've been shot!'

I dropped down by his side and put my hands over my ears. I wanted to drown out the terrible shriek of the enemy bomber. A Stuka it was, with whistles on its wings that made a screeching noise when the plane went into a dive. Now it climbed away, engine growling. It looked dark against the blue sky. It was the German plane that people feared and hated most of all.

I lifted my head and looked at Freddo curled up on the floor of the *gwli*. He was still clutching his neck but he'd stopped moaning.

'Where've you been hit, Fred?' I got onto my knees and tried to pull his hand away so I could see the damage. 'Where'd he get you?'

There was a little trickle of blood behind his left ear, making his hair go all sticky red. Slowly he sat up and touched the wound. He made a bit of a face and sounded off a string of Italian words. Swearwords, probably.

Then we heard someone laughing.

'Who's that?' I shouted. 'What's there to laugh at?'

A head popped up behind the low wall at the side of the *gwli*.

Ivor Ingrams. He was in his back garden. With some friends by the sound of it, because there were more laughs from behind the wall.

'God, you're *twp* you two,' Ivor smirked. 'Stupid.'

Freddo was on his feet now, angry. I scrambled up to stand at his side. We didn't like Ivor Ingrams. He was a bully, see. Especially to Freddo's brother, Aldo.

Aldo was older than us. He was a bit on the slow side, though, so we kept an eye on him, minded him.

'Who you calling *twp*?' Freddo squared up to face the wall. A little drop of blood spotted his shirt collar.

'Who d'you think, *Eyetie*? You!'

There was more laughter at that. 'Eyeties' was the nasty name that some people called the Italians who lived in our village.

Then more heads popped up, three of the English evacuees who'd come to live here because of the war with Germany. Ivor had made friends with them. They were his best butties now, not us Welsh boys.

'You didn't get hit by a bullet, *twpsyn*! I copped you with a stone.'

The boys behind the wall laughed louder when Ivor said this. One of them put his hand to his head. 'Owwwwww. I've been shot, I have. Owwww.'

The others joined in, jeering and laughing. One of them staggered around a bit, pretending he'd been wounded too.

I thought Freddo was going to explode, do something mad like jump the wall and take them all on. 'Let's go, Fred,' I whispered, but not quiet enough.

6

'Aw, they're going home to their mummies,' one of the evacuees called out. 'Little Robert and his Italian friend.'

'Shut up, you!' Freddo yelled back. He made a move towards them, tamping mad. He was ready for a fight.

Ivor climbed up on the wall. He was ready too.

The evacuees egged him on. 'Teach 'im a lesson, mate.'

'Great Britain v Italy. Show 'im who's boss.'

Ivor jumped down into the *gwli*, but no sooner had his feet touched the ground than Freddo charged. Though Ivor was a lot bigger than us two, the force of Freddo's attack knocked him back against the wall.

Then he got his balance and lashed out at Freddo, who came spinning towards me, knocking me sideways.

The evacuees came leaping over the wall, shouting, excited.

Freddo charged again, roaring with anger, Italian words we didn't understand.

This time Ivor was ready for him. As Freddo got close, he reached out and grabbed him round the neck. He was big enough and strong enough to pin Freddo to the spot.

The English boys gathered round and laughed as Ivor tried to force Freddo to his knees.

Ivor looked over at me. 'In' you going to help your *Eyetie* friend, Rob?' he said, puffing a bit, trying to keep hold of Freddo. 'Come on. I thought you was best butties.'

No point in lying: I was scared of Ivor Ingrams, big bully that he was. Maybe if I ran at him fast, I could knock him off balance again, and then he'd let go. So I charged, my heart bumping in my chest.

One of the evacuees ran to stop me and grabbed hold of my arm. I tried to wrestle free, but I couldn't.

Then, above all the noise and commotion, there came a huge explosion.

BOOMPH!

The fighting stopped, straight off. Ivor let go of Freddo. The evacuee let go of my arm. We stood and listened, out of breath, panting.

'What was that?' someone said.

The sound had come from nearby.

'It's a bomb!' said Ivor. 'That Stuka's dropped a bomb.'

Then we heard the sound of gunfire too.

'Let's go and look!' someone else shouted and suddenly we didn't have to fight any more. We all had to go and see what had happened.

'Sounds like it was Blaenfelin way,' said Ivor.

'Not as far as that,' grunted Freddo. 'Over by the Huts, more like. Come on!'

And with that, the whole gang of us pelted off down the *gwli*.

Chapter 2

Past the church we went, by the picture house, down the hill that led to the pit.

The Huts were a bit further along the valley. They were just wooden shacks really, but people still lived in them. My nanna said that they were put up a long time ago for the workers who'd built the mine.

As we ran we saw loads of people out on their doorsteps. 'Where did the bomb drop, boys?' someone shouted.

'Get off the street, you idiots,' shouted someone else. 'They may be dropping more. Go home to your mams. They'll be worried.'

We didn't stop to listen. We raced on full pelt and now we were joined by other kids.

My butties, Vic and Billy, came racing along Cardiff Road.

'Where you going, Rob?' Billy yelled, trying to catch up with me.

'Down the Huts,' I gasped, running backwards as I waited for him to draw level.

I was excited – we all were – but a bit scared too. What if the Stuka came back, diving and shooting, with another stack of bombs? Perhaps the people on the doorsteps were right to warn us.

We'd been having daylight raids for a few weeks now in our part of south Wales. Sometimes the siren would sound a warning. Then you'd take cover under the stairs or run for the Anderson shelters people were building in their gardens. Sometimes, like today, the siren didn't sound, so the first you knew was when the planes came shrieking out of the sky.

Mind you, there'd never been a raid this close before. It felt like the war had really started for us, even though it had been going on for nearly a year.

The sound of a bell came clanging along the street. We were down by the pit wall by now, a big gang of kids and a few grown-ups, all running, all chopsing away.

'It's the fire engine,' yelled Freddo.

'There's quick!' said Vic, impressed.

The bright red truck rattled closer, bell ringing. Inside, we could see some of the firemen struggling into their uniforms.

We shouted and cheered and pressed ourselves along the wall as the engine rattled by.

'There's my Uncle Tecwyn,' Billy shouted, pointing at the man behind the wheel.

'Come on, Uncle Tecwyn!' we yelled. 'Put your foot down.'

As if he heard us, the engine revved and sped on. We closed in behind, running to catch up.

The Huts were only a little way further on from the pit. When we came round the corner of the wall we could see them in the dip of the road. They were just two lines of little wooden houses facing each other, no upstairs rooms.

Freddo was right. This is where the bomb – or bombs – had dropped. Perhaps they'd been aiming for the pit. By the look of it, the street had copped a direct hit, because one of the rows of houses had a great splintery hole in the middle. Smoke curled up in the air but there didn't seem to be much of a fire to put out.

We ran down the dip, wanting to get closer and see more. A policeman came puffing up the hill, waving his arms, trying to stop us. Gethin Richards it was, our local bobby.

'Nothing to see here, boys. Nothing to see.' He was red-faced and sweating. 'Why in't you in school, anyway?'

'School's over,' Ivor said.

We dodged round PC Richards and got closer to where the bomb had dropped. Now we could see the damage more closely. The house that had been hit was just a heap of shattered wood and broken slates. Bits of furniture were sticking out of the rubble. A clock and a cushion and a birdcage were perched on top. No bird though, just a few feathers. A tin washing-up bowl had landed in the street, right where the front door had been. The dishes were still piled up inside, none of them broken by the look of it. Not one!

A little crowd stood and watched as the firemen began to dig through the rubble. 'No one home, thank God,' somebody said.

We were quiet now, shocked by what we saw. Then a voice piped up behind us. 'Mrs Parry got hit.'

It was Gwenda Lewis. 'She was running for the air-raid shelter in her garden and got knocked down by the blast. My father's taken her to hospital in his car.'

Gwenda was our local know-all. She always seemed to be there when anything exciting happened.

'How'd your father get here so quick, then?' Ivor asked.

'We were driving past just after the bomb dropped,' said Gwenda. 'A few seconds earlier and we could have been hit too! We had a lucky escape.'

'Pity,' Vic whispered, loud enough to make us laugh.

A man came out of a house down the street. He was white with dust from head to toe and wearing his pyjamas. Everyone turned to look at him. Some of the kids started laughing.

'I got blown out of bed!' he shouted. 'Comes to something when a man can't get his sleep.'

'Poor Hughie,' said one of the women nearby. 'He's working nights, in' he? Needs his rest.'

Then someone else shouted back, 'The missus says she can't never get you out of bed, Hugh. Sent a Stuka to wake you up!'

People laughed and the man shook his fist at us. Then he shuffled off back inside his house, muttering under his breath.

'Right then: time to go home now.' PC Richards was back on the scene. 'Nothing more to look at.'

'My father said to wait here for him, Mr Richards.' That was Gwenda.

'You go off home, there's a good girl. I'll tell your father when he gets here.'

'But he said . . .' Gwenda carried on, as usual, but PC Richards wasn't having any of it.

'Go home,' he said, 'with the rest of them. Let these men do their work.' He took off his helmet and wiped his brow as the fireman began pulling planks of wood from the wreckage.

All of a sudden, Freddo bent down and picked something up from the rubble by his feet.

'What you doing, Frederico?' PC Richards gave him a look. (Frederico was Freddo's proper name.)

'Checking my shoelace is tied, Mr Richards.' Freddo straightened up, looking a bit sheepish. He kept one hand clenched tight behind his back. 'That's all.'

'Oh aye,' said PC Richards, not believing. 'Well you'd better go home and get yourself cleaned up.' He pointed to the dried blood on Freddo's face and collar. 'Looks like you been in the wars.'

He gave a little laugh at his own joke and walked away to see what the firemen were up to.

Ivor was standing near enough to hear what PC Richards had said. He called across to Freddo: 'Aye. And the war's not over yet, is it, butt? Got a fight to finish off, you and me!'

'Any time you like,' Freddo yelled back, putting on a brave face. Then he turned to me. 'Come on, Rob.' He elbowed some of the evacuees out of the way and broke into a run. 'Let's go home and tell Aldo.'

Chapter 3

We didn't go straight to his house, though. Freddo said he wanted to go down the Glan. 'Got something to show you, Rob. It's more secret down by there.'

The Glan was the name of a little valley below the railway embankment. At this time of year, the banks were covered in thick ferns, nearly tall enough to hide kids like us.

Freddo led the way along the path that followed the stream at the bottom of the valley. It had been boiling hot for weeks, but there was always water down by the Glan because it came from the Pandy Pool, higher up.

We ducked and dodged the green fern leaves where they got in our way.

'What you got in your hand, Fred?' I reached out and grabbed his shoulder, making him slow down. I couldn't wait any longer to find out what he was hiding. 'Let's see.'

Freddo stopped and looked up and down the path to check whether anyone else was about.

Then he twtied down on the path and made me do the same. Slow as a snail and enjoying the drama, he opened his hand. In his palm was a little piece of silver metal. Flat it was, and shaped like a mushroom.

I whistled, very impressed. I didn't know what I was looking at, though.

'It's a German bullet,' said Freddo, very quiet, as if there could be spies around. 'My Uncle Antony showed me one, once.' His Uncle Antony was in the Royal Air Force. He often brought Freddo interesting things to look at.

'I know what it is,' I said. I didn't want to let on I'd never seen one before.

'They get flattened when they hit the ground,' said Freddo. He held the bullet up between his fingers for us both to see it better. 'That Stuka must have been firing at the Huts before it dropped the bomb.'

'Why you so secret about it, Fred?'

'I didn't want anyone else to see, did I? You can get money for these, Uncle Antony says.'

'How much?'

'A penny.'

I whistled. A penny was a lot of money.

'That's what Uncle Antony told me, anyway,' said Freddo, giving the bullet a quick rub on his shorts. 'Have I still got blood on my face?'

'Yes,' I said. 'And it's on your shirt too.'

Freddo grunted. 'Better try and wash it off before Mamma sees.' He shoved the bullet in his pocket and crawled to the side of the stream. He cupped his hands together and dipped them. 'That's nice,' he said, as he brought the water up to his face. 'Fresh.'

With a second handful, he scrubbed his face clean. 'Show me where it got on my shirt, Rob.' He couldn't see where it had dribbled down his neck onto the collar.

'It's by here, Fred.'

I was just about to point it out to him when a loud crashing sound came from the top of the embankment.

We looked up, startled. My heart started banging.

The sound came nearer. Something was tumbling down the bank through the ferns.

'Blinking hell!' I jumped to my feet. Freddo was up too, dripping water, cursing in Italian.

Whatever it was kept on rolling through the ferns.

'It's a bomb,' Freddo shouted. 'Run for it!'

But then we heard another shout, high up on the embankment. 'Damn and blast!' It was a girl's voice, sounding like it was coming from the path that ran by the railway fence. 'Damn and blast.'

Freddo and me were rooted to the spot and then the 'bomb' suddenly burst out of the ferns and landed at our feet.

It was a suitcase. A big, brown, battered suitcase.

Freddo shot out a foot to stop it doing another tumble into the water. 'Ouch!' he yelped. It was heavier than he thought. Then he shouted up the embankment. 'Oi! Watch what you're doing, will you?'

The girl shouted back. 'Sorry. Didn't do it on purpose.'

'You're dangerous, you are,' I yelled. 'Bad as a bloomin' Stuka.'

Freddo laughed. Me too. We were both a bit relieved, to tell the truth.

'Hang on. I'm coming down,' the girl shouted and there was more crashing about in the ferns. Black curls bobbing – that was all we could see of her as she scrambled down the slope.

When she finally appeared, there were bits of fern stuck to her clothes and her hair. 'Oh, I am sorry, boys,' she said. 'Did I frighten you?'

'No!' we lied.

She was much older than us. Aldo's age, maybe.

She was wearing a dress and a cardie, and her face was all flushed red. She bent down to see if the case was broken. 'Slipped out of my hand,' she said. 'Couldn't catch it when it started rolling.'

'What were you doing up there?' Freddo asked.

'I was on my way home,' said the girl. '*Duw*, it's hot.'

She tucked her dress around her knees and dropped down by the side of the stream. She splashed the cool water up onto her face and hair.

Freddo mouthed something at me. '*Let's go!*'

But before we could, the girl scooped a big gulp of water from the stream and stood up. She wiped her mouth with her hand. 'Oh, that's better.' She brushed the wet hair back off her face. 'My name's Elizabeth Morgan, but you can call me Lizzie if you like. What's yours?'

'Robert Prosser,' I said.

'Fred,' said Freddo.

'Fred what?'

Freddo glanced at me, sharpish. I wondered if he was a bit nervous to say his last name.

'Cat got your tongue?' the girl asked.

'No,' Freddo mumbled. 'It's Moretti.'

'Italian, are you?'

'Yes.'

'He was born here though,' I chipped in, fast.

'One of my best friends at school was Italian,' Elizabeth said. 'Her mam and dad sent her back to Italy when the war started.'

She straightened out her dress and went to pick up the suitcase. 'Have they been to take your father away then?' she asked Freddo, lifting the case as easy as anything.

'Yes,' said Freddo.

'Do you know where he is?'

'In England, somewhere,' said Freddo, sounding bitter. 'In a camp.'

Because Italy had come into the war on the German side, all Italian men were being kept under lock and key. They were our 'enemies' now, but I couldn't imagine Mr Moretti doing anything to harm us. He was kind and gentle, and he'd been living in Wales for ages. 'He's one of us, is Pietro,' my nanna was fond of saying.

'My Uncle Dino says there's a rumour that they might get sent away to Canada,' said Freddo. Uncle Dino was with Mr Moretti, but he had a phone at home, so sometimes he could make calls to Aunty Edda and tell her what was happening.

'Sorry to hear that,' said Elizabeth. 'I better be going though. Can I get to Mabon Road if I stay on this path?'

'Yes,' we said. Then Freddo asked, 'Where you going then? And why have you got that big case?'

'I'm going home,' she said. 'My father lives up near the Garth. On the Tŷ Cornant farm. Do you know it?'

We didn't, because it was high up on the hills above our village, and more towards the Cefn Du valley than ours. Which explains why we'd never seen this girl before.

'That's miles away,' I said. 'Why you walking from here?'

'Didn't have any choice, did I?' Elizabeth put the case down again. 'Usually I'd get off at Berw Junction but they stopped the train here. Wouldn't go any further. Someone

18

said there's a German plane attacking the railway tracks higher up the valley.'

'He was bombing us earlier,' said Freddo.

'Got a direct hit,' I added. 'On the Huts.'

'There's terrible,' said Elizabeth. 'Hope no one was killed?'

'No,' I said. 'Where have you come from?'

She laughed then. 'You ask a lot of questions.'

'Well, you could be a spy for all we know,' said Freddo.

We'd been told to be on the lookout for any strangers, because we'd heard that the Germans might parachute people in, maybe disguised as nuns, or nurses. We had to be on our guard at all times.

'You're right. I could be,' said the girl. 'But I'm not.' She suddenly took off her shoes. 'My feet are killing me, so I'm going to dip them in the stream.'

She sat down at the side of the Glan, cooling off her feet in the water. We did too, and that's where we learnt all about her. She was sixteen and she'd been working away in London as a servant. 'A big house in Notting Hill,' she said. 'Have you heard of it?'

We hadn't.

'Lovely it was,' she went on. 'The house, I mean. Not the people. Right load of snobs.'

So when her father said he wanted her home to help on the farm now that most of his men had gone off to fight, she was only too happy to come.

'And I think he was a bit afraid that London was going to get bombed,' Elizabeth said. 'He thought it would be safer here. Not so sure now after what you told me.'

'We haven't had many raids,' said Freddo. 'Single planes, mostly.'

'I'll have to make sure I keep dodging them then.' Elizabeth got up and tried to wipe her wet feet with a hanky she pulled out of her pocket. 'I better get going or Daddy will be starting to worry.' She squeezed into her shoes.

'Where's your mam, then?' I asked.

'Oh, she died when I was little.'

We didn't know what to say to that.

'It was a long time ago,' said Elizabeth. 'These things happen.' She grabbed hold of the case handle. 'You should come and visit us at the farm,' she said. 'We still got some animals.'

'Great!' said Freddo. 'Aldo would like that.'

'Who's Aldo?' Elizabeth asked.

'My big brother. He's sixteen.'

'Oh good. Someone for me to have a proper talk to, instead of little kids like you.' She laughed when she said it, so we knew she didn't mean it. Besides, she didn't know what Aldo was like. Sometimes it was difficult to have a sensible conversation with him.

'Ta-ta then, boys.' She set off along the path with the big brown case bumping along by her side. Then she turned to call back. 'Come and see us at the farm. Promise?'

'Promise,' I shouted back.

'What's the time now?' Freddo asked, yanking his feet out of the stream.

Elizabeth had a watch. 'Nearly six,' she shouted.

'Oh, heck!' I jumped up and tried to shove my wet feet into my daps. 'My mam'll kill me!'

Freddo jumped up too. 'We better get going.' Then he yelled up the path: 'See you, Lizzie!'

Chapter 4

I was heading for real trouble.

See, when my mam was working a long shift at the factory, I had to get Nanna's tea ready. She was nearly blind, so making her food was one of my jobs.

Dad was away fighting, so he couldn't help.

If I didn't hurry up, Nanna would be kept waiting and that wouldn't make her very happy. She liked her food.

My mam wouldn't be very happy either. I might end up with a clip on the head if I wasn't careful.

We ran like mad, feet still squelching wet in our daps.

'Where's the fire, boys?' Mr Yoxall passed us on his way from the pit, face black with coal dust.

'Nowhere,' I shouted.

But Freddo said, 'Down by the Huts!' Then he stopped dead and pointed along the street. 'There's my Aunty Edda. She must be going to our shop.'

Freddo's family kept one of the cafés in our village.

Moretti's Café sold coffees and teas and sweets and chocolates and, best of all, ice cream in cornets and wafers. Mr Moretti made it in a shed at the back of the shop. Well, he used to make it before the war, but he hadn't been able to since they'd brought in rationing. Now things like sugar were hard to get.

Anyway, the café had been closed since Mr Moretti was taken away. 'For stocktaking,' Mrs Moretti said.

But my nanna said it was because of something different.

'She hasn't got the heart to keep it going. Not with Pietro being away and people being so nasty. Poor Lena.'

It was true that since Italy had gone into the war on Germany's side, some people had taken against all the Italian shopkeepers. 'Enemy aliens' they called them.

'The Morettis have been living here for years,' Nanna would mutter. 'They're as much a part of this village as you and me.'

Not everyone thought like that, though, so Mrs Moretti had decided to close down for a while. Perhaps she hoped that all the bad feeling would soon blow over.

'Aunty Edda!' Freddo shouted.

She didn't hear him, or didn't want to. She was in a big hurry. Small and dumpy, she was running along as fast as her little legs would carry her.

'Aunty!' Freddo called again and we set off to catch her up. 'What's the matter?'

Now she stopped and turned round, and we could see she was crying. Her face was all puffed up and her eyes were red and sore. 'Frederico!' She ran back towards us, one hand stretched out to grab Freddo's arm.

'What is it, Aunty?' he asked. 'Bad news?'

'Not here. I can't tell you here. In the street.' She was pulling him along towards the shop. I followed behind, but she didn't even seem to notice me.

The shop door was closed and Aunty Edda started banging on it. Now she was gabbling something to Freddo in Italian. He gabbled back, but he didn't bother to translate for me like he usually did.

Through the glass in the door, we could see Mrs Moretti scurrying through the shop from the kitchen at the back. Aldo was with her. Even from where we were, you could see the worried look on his face.

'I better be going,' I said, as Mrs Moretti unlocked the front door and almost pulled Aunty Edda inside.

Freddo held onto my arm. 'No, don't, Rob. Hang on a minute.'

Aunty Edda stumbled in through the door, still crying, and talking fast as anything to Mrs Moretti.

'I'm going to be late, Fred.'

I tried to pull my arm away but, strong and fierce, Freddo gripped even tighter. 'Only for a bit, Rob. You're my best friend, in' you?'

'Aye, but I'm going to get in dead trouble if I'm late.'

'Please!' He was almost begging. The others had gone through the shop, talking, talking.

Mrs Pritchard, four doors down, came out to see what the commotion was. 'More trouble is it, Frederico?' she called up the street. She was enjoying the drama.

'No!' Freddo snarled back. 'And it's none of your business, anyway.'

With that he pulled me inside the shop. I knew why he wanted me there. He was afraid there was bad news coming and he wanted a friend to be around when it all came out. In wartime there was always a lot of bad news.

We went through into the kitchen. Usually, I liked coming here. It was cosy and full of colour, not like our dark old kitchen at home. There were pictures on the walls, scenes of mountains and lakes and beaches on the edge of blue, blue seas. There was a big comfy couch too and a round table covered with a red cloth.

Mrs Moretti and Aldo were sitting at the table with Aunty Edda. She'd stopped crying now, but she was dabbing at her eyes and mouth with her hanky. Mrs Moretti sat still as anything, but her face was chalk-white and her eyes looked frightened.

Big, gentle Aldo was whimpering very quietly. His dark eyes were as scared-looking as his mother's. She was stroking his hand.

Me and Freddo stood by the door and listened as Aunty Edda tried to get her breath back. I was embarrassed to be there, but when Freddo butted in to ask if it was all right, Mrs Moretti nodded. 'Of course. Robert is a good friend to our family. Now, Edda, tell us what you've heard.'

'It was on the wireless, Lena.' Aunty Edda was still out of breath and still trying not to cry.

'Yes, you said,' Mrs Moretti went on. 'What exactly?'

'It was on the news. There's a ship been sunk on its way to Canada.' And now Aunty Edda couldn't stop the tears. 'Oh, Lena. It was carrying Italian internees.'

'Internees' was what they called the men that had been rounded up and taken to camps. Like Mr Moretti.

Aldo burst into tears. 'Papa's on that ship,' he said. 'I know it.'

'Quiet, now,' said his mam. 'No need to cry. We don't know exactly *where* Papa is. Save your tears for later.' And she stroked his hand more firmly. 'Tell us what else they said on the wireless, Edda.'

So, standing there in the kitchen doorway, I learnt

what the trouble was. Sometimes they spoke in English, sometimes in Italian but when that happened Freddo translated for me.

A ship called the *Arandora Star* had set sail from Liverpool. It was packed with Italians and Germans and was heading for Canada.

'Why was it going to Canada?' Aldo snuffled.

'Canada's one of our Dominions, Al,' Freddo explained. 'It belongs to the King. Like Australia.'

Off the coast of Ireland, the ship had been hit by a single torpedo from a German submarine. It had sunk in less than forty minutes. Hundreds of people had drowned.

When Aunty Edda told us this bit, she gave a great big sob and the tears poured down her cheeks more than ever. Aldo laid his head on the table and pressed his hands to his ears. His body was shaking.

Freddo had gone as chalk-white as his mam, but he didn't cry.

Then Mrs Moretti said, 'Where did they come from, Edda?' She looked calm, but her voice wobbled a little bit when she spoke. 'Which camps? Did they say?'

'No.' Aunty Edda dabbed her eyes with a hanky. 'They just said that the ship was full of Fascists and Nazis.'

'There you are, then!' Mrs Moretti clapped her hands. 'Our men couldn't have been on board. They're not Fascists!'

Aldo raised his head from the table. 'What're you saying, Mamma? I don't understand.'

So Mrs Moretti told him. 'Fascists follow people like Hitler and Mussolini. Dictators. Bullies! Always telling people what to think and do.'

Hitler was the German leader. Mussolini was the leader of Italy.

'Papa never had any time for the likes of them,' Mrs Moretti said. 'So you see, lovely boy, he couldn't have been on that ship.'

'Nor Uncle Dino?'

'Nor Uncle Dino. They're both good men.'

Aunty Edda sniffed and swallowed and gave a little smile. 'They *are* good men. Loyal to this country, too. They wouldn't get sent away with a bunch of Fascists.' She put her wet hanky in her handbag. 'How about a cup of tea, Lena?'

'I'll make it!' Freddo moved to the stove, glad of something to do. 'You having one, Rob?'

'No thanks, Fred. I gotta go now. Nanna will be getting hungry.'

Aldo laughed. 'She loves her food, your nanna.'

I laughed too, more out of relief than anything. But all I wanted was to get away. Fast!

Chapter 5

'Where the hell have you been?'

My mam was banging pots and pans around on the stove in our kitchen. 'I was worried stiff you might have been in that raid.'

'No, I been . . .'

I couldn't get the rest of it out, because Nanna chipped in from her big chair next to the sideboard and the wireless. An organist was playing. Because my nanna couldn't see very well, she spent a lot of time sitting in the kitchen, listening to the wireless. 'My stomach thinks my throat have been cut,' she said. Just to ram the message home.

'Sorry, Mam,' I gulped. 'I didn't think you'd be home yet.'

I went to help her.

She handed me some carrots. 'Peel those. And don't go wasting any.'

I took them over to the sink and started scraping the skins, careful not to take too much off.

'Well, where *have* you been?' Mam went on. 'Not the Pandy Pool, I hope.'

'No. We haven't been over there since Reg went away.'

Reg had been our evacuee. He'd come from Kent with the other boys from his school. One day, he'd got into a bit of a fight with us up at the Pandy and nearly drowned. That's why my mam didn't want me going there.

'Aw, Reginald,' Nanna said. 'I do miss him.' My nan had a soft spot for Reg. She didn't know how mean he was. I was glad when his mam had come to take him home.

'I been with the Morettis,' I said. 'Their Aunty Edda came over to tell them about a ship that got torpedoed on the way to Canada.'

'That's true, that is,' said Nanna. 'I heard it on the news, Myra. Full of Italians and Germans, they say.'

'*Duw, Duw,*' said my mother, putting some potatoes in a pan. 'I hope Pietro wasn't on board.'

'They don't think he could have been,' I said, and I told them what Mrs Moretti had said about the ship being full of Fascists and how Mr Moretti wasn't a Fascist. 'And Uncle Dino isn't either,' I finished off.

Then I was sent upstairs to put up the blackout curtains so that we could have the gas lamps on. You had to have the windows covered over at night so that enemy bombers wouldn't be able to spot any signs of light.

In my mam's bedroom, I stood on a chair and fastened the thick black cloth to the hooks at the top of the window frame. Then I did the same in Nanna's room.

In my room, I could stand on the spare bed to fix the curtains. This was the bed that Reg had slept in. Not having him around any more made me feel happy. I did a little bounce on the mattress to celebrate.

When I came back downstairs, Mam had just finished putting up the blackout curtains on the kitchen windows. She was still talking to Nanna about the *Arandora Star*. Then they got round to talking about Dad and how we didn't know where he was and how it made it worse, not knowing.

He'd been fighting with the Navy in Norway, but our ships had pulled out of there now. The ones that hadn't been sunk, that is. Some of the sailors had come home already. We'd seen their pictures in the paper. Not my dad, though, and we hadn't had any letters from him for weeks and weeks. We didn't even know which ship he was on.

'Look on the bright side, Myra,' said Nanna. 'We'd most likely have heard if he'd been ki–'

She'd been going to say 'killed' but changed it quickly to 'We'd have heard if he was in any trouble'.

That was true. People got a telegram from the Admiralty when a relative was 'missing'. Or 'lost in action' as they put it.

'Oh, Mam, don't you go giving me that *No news is good news* stuff,' my mother went on. 'I get that all the time at work.'

She pushed her chair back noisily and stretched up to light the gas lamp. *HISSSSSS* went the gas as she turned on the little tap at the side of the mantle. She put a match to it and the room slowly filled with yellow light.

Then she sat down again and lit a cigarette. Behind her, the pans on the stove bubbled away. 'What I want,' she said, 'is for Tom to be home, safe.'

'Me too,' I said, getting knives and forks out of the sideboard drawer. I brought them over to the table.

'Of course you do,' said my mam. She reached up to ruffle my hair. That didn't happen very often.

'We all want him home,' said Nanna. 'Now, when's that dinner going to be ready?'

Chapter 6

'What we gonna do today then?' Freddo asked.

We were sitting on the stone wall of the Glan bridge, just by where Maesgwyn Road crossed over the stream.

Freddo chucked a stone into the water. It copped a branch that was floating by.

'Good shot, Fred!' Aldo gave his brother a great big smack on the back. 'Direct hit.'

Freddo wobbled a bit on the wall and grabbed hold of my arm. 'Watch it, Al,' he shouted. 'You'll have me in the water, mun.'

I yelled out too, because I thought Freddo could have pulled me off the ledge with him. 'Go easy, Al. You don't know your own strength, you don't!'

'Sorry, Rob,' said Aldo. 'Didn't mean to give you a fright.'

'Well, you did,' said Freddo, getting his balance back. 'You don't think sometimes, you don't.'

'Sorry,' Aldo said again, and made like he was going to give his brother a hug.

'Don't!' said Freddo. 'Just sit quiet for a bit.'

So we all did. For a bit. Just watching the water, enjoying the afternoon sun.

We were on our way back from Maesgwyn. In the night, there'd been another air raid and bombs had been dropped. A lorry driving along in the blackout had fallen down one of the craters. That's what people were saying, anyway.

By the time we'd got there, though, the lorry had been lifted out and there wasn't much to see. Just a big hole in the road. No souvenirs, either, like the bullet that Freddo had found down by the Huts. Other kids had got there before us!

Aldo was the most disappointed. He'd brought a big bag with him. It looked like it was made out of an old brown sack. It had a string to tie up the top, and another one to hook it over your shoulder. Aldo said his dad had brought it with him from Italy a long time ago.

'It reminds me of him,' Aldo had said, 'now that he's gone away.' He'd got a bit teary when he said this, but then he'd brightened up. 'And it's big, see, Rob. So when we find stuff, we'll be able to carry it home in the bag. Lots!'

It had looked a bit full to me when we'd set out, but Aldo wouldn't say what was inside. I thought it might be his gas mask, but he just laughed. We were all supposed to carry our gas masks, in case of an enemy gas attack, but not many people did.

The bag was slung over his shoulder now, dangling over the edge of the bridge.

'So?' repeated Freddo. 'What we gonna do then?'

'We could go up the Pandy Pool,' said Aldo. 'Have a swim, like. Play games.'

Freddo and me looked at each other. 'I don't think we want to go up there, Al,' I said.

The truth was that the games we used to play most up the Pandy were usually about German submarines firing at our ships. That didn't feel like fun any more. Not now we'd heard the news about the *Arandora Star*.

We still hadn't been told if Mr Moretti had been on board. Mrs Moretti kept putting on a brave face, telling the boys that their father wouldn't have been there 'with all those Fascists'.

But the truth was that she didn't really know. She couldn't seem to get any more information, no matter how hard she tried. Someone said to write a letter to the Shipping and Seamen Office in Cardiff. So she did, but she hadn't got a reply yet. The worry was nibbling away at them all, I could tell.

Freddo sighed. 'Al, we don't feel like playing games up the Pandy. I don't, anyway.'

'Not games like we used to, Al,' I said.

'Right you are,' he said, a bit sad.

Voices came echoing down the road. A group of kids. We couldn't see them because the hedge was too high.

'Sounds like Vic and Billy,' said Freddo.

Then a girl's voice cut in.

'And Gwenda Lewis,' I said. 'Worse luck.'

Aldo laughed. He'd cheered up again now.

The three came round the corner by the telegraph pole.

'Hiya,' Billy shouted when he saw us. He raced ahead of the others and jumped up on the ledge of the bridge. 'What you doing then?'

'What's it look like?' said Freddo. 'Nothin'.'

'Same as usual, then.' That was Gwenda. She was carrying her gas mask in a box hanging on a string round her shoulder. Trust her!

'Ha, ha!' Freddo went. 'Not very funny. *As usual*!'

'What you got in the bag?' Billy pointed at Aldo.

'Not a lot,' said Aldo.

'Not your gas mask, then?' smirked Gwenda.

'None of your business,' said Freddo.

I could see that Gwenda was just about to start on one of her little lectures about how everyone should always carry their gas mask with them when Vic chipped in: 'We been to Maesgwyn.'

'So have we,' said Aldo.

'We didn't see you,' I added.

'Didn't see you either,' said Vic.

'Did you go with her?' Freddo nodded at Gwenda.

'Not exactly,' Billy said.

'I went with my father,' said Gwenda, 'but he had to go off on official business.'

'Official business.' Vic winked at us. 'There's posh!'

Gwenda ignored him. 'I saw these two and tagged along with them. They're coming back to my house.'

'Your house!' Freddo jumped down off the wall, hardly believing what he was hearing. 'What you going to her house for, boys?'

Billy and Vic looked a bit sheepish, but Gwenda put on one of her superior looks and said, 'We've got our own Anderson shelter now. They're coming to see it.'

Anderson shelters were popping up all over the place. They were like little sheds made of corrugated iron. You sunk them down into a hole in your garden. If you had a garden, that is. They were supposed to protect you from bomb blast, but some people said they felt safer in their own houses.

33

'Wouldn't get me in one of those things,' my nanna had said. 'Like digging your own coffin.'

'My father finished building it yesterday,' Gwenda went on. 'It's got bunk beds . . .'

'And a 'lectric fire,' said Vic, impressed.

'You three can come and see it if you want,' Gwenda said.

'Yes please,' said Aldo, slowly lowering himself off the wall, holding onto his father's bag. 'I never been in an Anderson shelter.'

None of us had. So, even though it was Gwenda's, I knew I wanted to see it.

I knew that Freddo did too, but what he said was, 'Suppose so. I got to keep an eye on Aldo, see.'

Gwenda smirked a bit. 'Of course you have. He's so little, isn' he? Can't mind himself, poor thing.'

Aldo thought that was funny, but Freddo just scowled. 'Come on then,' he said. 'I haven't got time to hang around.'

Chapter 7

Gwenda's house was up Williams Terrace, near the park.

It was posher than our house. It stood all by itself in its own garden, with steps up to the front door.

Gwenda led the way round the side of the house. They had a little gate that opened into their back garden. She was still chopsin' on about how snug and comfy they'd be in their new shelter, with her mam making cups of tea and toasting bread on the electric fire.

'Will your mam mind us coming here, then?' Billy asked.

'She's not in,' said Gwenda. 'She's at the Red Cross shop, sorting clothes. She's in charge.'

'She would be!' Freddo muttered.

Gwenda led us into the garden.

Vic whistled. 'Big!'

It was too.

'Nearly as big as the park,' said Billy, impressed.

We all were. There was a small grass lawn, but most of the space was given over to growing vegetables. That's what people did if they had a garden. 'Dig for Victory' was what the government kept saying.

'My father grows most of our food,' said Gwenda, marching along the path to the far wall.

We looked at each other and rolled our eyes.

At the end of the garden was a big mound of earth. This was where they'd sunk the shelter into the ground.

The corrugated iron roof curved above the lawn and the earth was banked up along the sides and top to give it more protection against a bomb blast. There were vegetables newly planted on the roof.

Three steps dropped down to the little doorway. The opening was covered by a thick blanket. Gwenda pulled it to one side and reached in to switch on the light. 'I'll put the electric fire on,' she said. 'Just to show you.'

'My Uncle Tecwyn says people in't supposed to have electric light in their shelters,' said Billy. 'A bomb might cut the cable and start a fire. He should know. He's a fireman.'

'Well,' said Gwenda, all hoity-toity, 'my father's the air-raid warden, isn't he, so *he* should know too. Are you coming in or not?' She shuffled into the shelter.

Billy followed her. He turned and winked at us as he went in. 'Won't just be the bread that gets toasted if the cable gets cut!'

Freddo and Vic and me laughed and followed.

Aldo looked puzzled. 'What else they toasting, Fred?'

'Nothing, Al. Just a joke,' said Freddo and reached out a hand to help him down the steps. Aldo had a bit of trouble getting into the shelter because he was so big and the doorway was so narrow. He clutched his bag to his chest and squeezed in.

He had to bend down, though, like the rest of us because the walls were curved and not very high.

'Sit down, then,' said Gwenda. 'Make more room.'

We did as we were told, but it was a tight fit. Along each side of the shelter were narrow benches, with blankets and pillows all ready for sleeping on. At the end was a little electric fire and a cupboard. The walls were painted white. A dim glow came from the light bulb fixed to the ceiling. And that was it.

We sat huddled up on the benches, hands on knees because there was nowhere else to put them.

Me and Vic and Gwenda sat on one side. Freddo and Billy sat on the other, squashed up to the end walls by Aldo, who was sitting hunched in the middle. His bag was on his lap.

Gwenda went on about how they'd be able to come down to the shelter in an air raid, and how much safer they'd feel than if they stayed in the house. She switched the electric fire on and off to show it was working. We were all impressed but didn't want to let on.

'What do you think of it, then?' she asked.

'Tidy,' said Vic.

'Bit small,' said Billy.

'It smells,' said Aldo.

Vic giggled.

'Of what?' Gwenda asked, all hurt.

'I dunno,' said Aldo. 'It does though, don' it, Fred?'

'Yes, Al, it does,' said Freddo.

'*Of what*?' Gwenda went on, more pushy now.

'Of damp,' said Freddo. 'It smells of damp.'

'That's because it's new,' snapped Gwenda.

'It's because part of it is under the ground,' said Billy. 'The earth will be a bit wet.'

We all tried to look down at the floor but we couldn't really move very much.

'There's proper wooden planks,' said Gwenda.

'Aye, but the earth'll be damp underneath,' Billy went on.

Gwenda pouted a bit. 'Suppose that's something else your Uncle Tecwyn told you, is it?'

'No,' said Billy, and left it at that.

We all sat up straight again. No one spoke for a bit, then Freddo asked, 'Is it very dark in here with the light off?'

'Yes,' said Gwenda, and she flicked the switch.

It was pitch black to start with, but after a while you could see tiny bits of light coming round the blanket covering the door and from the chinks in the walls between the corrugated iron sheets. A bit like stars.

'*Ooooooooooo!*' went Billy in a ghostly voice.

'*Ooooooooooo!*' went the rest of us.

'Don't be silly, you boys.' Gwenda switched the light on.

'You frightened, Gwen?' I asked.

'Course not,' she said.

'Prove it,' Freddo teased. 'See how long we can all sit here in the dark.'

'All right,' said Gwenda. 'Won't worry me. Honest!'

She switched off the light.

'*Ooooooooooo!*' we all went.

Gwenda sniffed. 'Don't think you're scaring me, 'cos you're not!' Then she screamed. 'What's that?'

She switched the light on again. 'It's you, Victor Fletcher,' she said, smacking him on the arm.

'What's he doing then?' I asked.

'He was tickling me on the leg,' she said, offended.

'*Duw*, you're brave, Vic,' said Billy, and the rest of us laughed, especially Aldo. He thought it was really funny.

'Just wanted to give you a bit of a fright, Gwen,' said Vic, grinning.

'Did you think it was a *bwci-bo*?' Aldo asked, still laughing.

'Of course not,' Gwenda said. 'I knew it wasn't a ghost. Just one of you boys being silly.'

'Switch the light off again, Gwenda,' said Aldo. 'Show us you're not really scared.'

'All right. I will. Just to prove it.'

'For one minute,' said Freddo.

'All right. One minute. I'll count,' said Gwenda. 'But no silly nonsense, OK?'

'OK,' we muttered, but I don't know if we meant it.

Gwenda started counting. '*One, two, three . . .*'

We made a few more ghostly noises to begin with and then we sat quiet, trying to work out if we could see anything in the dark. Apart from Aldo who seemed to be shuffling around in his bag.

'*. . . twenty-seven, twenty-eight, twenty-nine . . .*'

Aldo shuffled around a bit more.

'Oi, Al, be careful,' said Billy. 'Mind my ribs.'

'Sorry, Bill,' Aldo whispered, and he giggled.

'What the hell are you up to, Al?' asked Freddo.

'Nothing, Fred.'

'*. . . forty-one, forty-two, forty-three . . .*'

'Ouch,' Billy yelped. 'Sit still, mun.'

'I will,' said Aldo, but the shuffling went on. It was like he was trying to pull something out of his bag.

'*. . . forty-nine, fifty . . .*'

'I've had enough of this,' Billy said. 'It's torture sitting next to him. Turn the light on.'

'*. . . fifty-five . . .*'

'HA HA HA HA HA HA!' Mad laughter came out of the darkness. Aldo! Loud it was, and scary.

Then a torch was flicked on and this big face with round staring eyes floated above us in the darkness.

'AHHHH!' we screamed, and wriggled in our seats.

'Switch the light on,' someone shouted.

Click! On it went. And there was Aldo holding up this big wooden puppet in one hand and shining a torch on its face with the other.

'Scared you!' He was shaking with laughter. 'I scared you all, didn't I, Fred? You thought it was a ghost.'

'No we didn't,' we all said, being brave now, though we'd all had a bit of a shock.

Aldo was making the puppet dance on his knees. It had spindly legs and a very long pointed nose. Its clothes were painted on, shorts and a jacket and a hat. There were strings to make it move. We all knew who it was supposed to be. We'd all been to see the Disney film.

'Pinocchio,' Vic whistled. 'Where d'you get it, Al?'

'It's Papa's,' said Aldo, very proud. 'He brought it with him from Italy. That's where Pinocchio comes from.' He jiggled the strings and made the puppet do another little dance.

'Put it back in the bag, Al.' Freddo's voice was very quiet.

'Aw, let him play with it a bit more,' said Billy.

'He's good at it,' said Vic.

'No!' Freddo looked angry. 'It's not his to play with.'

Aldo stopped jiggling the puppet. He wasn't laughing any more.

'There's no harm, Fred, is there?' I asked.

'I told you. It's not his.' Freddo was getting angrier. 'Papa said we must never play with it. Never! It's very old. It was given to him when he was a boy.'

'*Look, not touch*,' Aldo whispered. 'That's what Papa said.'

'Yes, Al,' said Freddo. '*Look, not touch*. So why did you bring it out of the house?'

'I wanted to have something of Papa's with me.' Aldo looked as if he was going to cry. 'It makes me feel he's a bit closer.' His eyes were filling with tears. The rest of us took shifty looks at each other, embarrassed.

'You had Papa's bag.' Freddo reached over to take the puppet from Aldo's hands. 'Wasn't that enough?'

'No,' said Aldo and now he did start to cry.

'We'd better be going,' Gwenda said, quick.

We all agreed.

Freddo was still trying to take the puppet from Aldo but Aldo wasn't letting go. 'Let me keep it, Fred.' He was almost sobbing now. 'I'll look after it. I won't break it.'

'No. Give it to me. I'll carry it home. Come on.' Freddo stood up.

Billy rubbed his shoulder and wriggled free while Gwenda fussed about with the pillows on the bench. Fred and Aldo were still tussling over the puppet.

Suddenly a great clattering sound came from the roof. RAT-A-TAT-A-TAT!

Again, RAT-A-TAT-A-TAT!!

We yelled and tried to drop to the floor, hands over our heads. It was a tight fit, though, and we couldn't really make it. We sat, crouched together in a heap, very scared.

'It's bullets,' someone shouted. 'We're being shot at!'

Chapter 8

The bullets stopped.

We didn't hardly dare breathe, still huddled together, heads down in the middle of the shelter.

'Switch the light off!' someone hissed.

Off it went.

It was dead silent after that until Billy whispered, 'I got something sharp sticking in my side.' Then a bit more panicky, 'It might be shrapnel.'

Shrapnel was the metal splinters from bombs or bullets.

Aldo whimpered.

We all shuffled about a bit to let Billy get at his wound. His elbow caught me in the face as he reached down to his side. Then he started giggling.

'It's the shock,' said Gwenda. 'He's going hysterical.'

'No I'm not,' said Billy, laughing more now, but not too loud.

'What's so funny then?' I asked. 'Can you feel the shrapnel? Are you bleeding?'

'It's not shrapnel,' Billy said, in fits of giggles. 'It's that puppet's nose. It's sticking in my ribs. It's bloomin' sharp, aye.'

We joined in the laughing, quietly. All except Freddo. I could tell in the darkness that he wasn't laughing. He was still angry with Aldo.

RAT-A-TAT-A-TAT!!!

We stopped laughing. Fast. And huddled together again in our little heap. We were waiting for the next attack.

In a while, Vic lifted his head and looked up at the roof. 'Can't be bullets,' he whispered. 'Bullets would rip through the metal. Leave holes.'

'You're right there, Vic,' I agreed.

'What is it then?' said Gwenda, a bit put out that she hadn't spotted this.

'It's stones, innit?' said Freddo. 'Someone's chucking stones on the roof.'

'Who'd do that?' asked Gwenda.

Me and Freddo nudged each other in the darkness. We had a good idea who.

'Ivor Ingrams and friends, that's who,' said Freddo. 'Come on. Let's go and find them!'

He stood up, a bit wobbly because we were all still tangled up in a heap. Aldo stood up too and that made it a bit easier for the rest of us to get on our feet. He was still holding onto the strings of his Pinocchio puppet.

'Cool head, Freddo,' Billy said, urgent. 'If we break cover, they'll just lob more stones at us.'

'We'll have to dodge them, then,' said Freddo.

'Weave in and out,' said Vic. 'Swerve around a bit.'

'Don't go treading on my father's vegetables,' warned Gwenda, getting up and shuffling towards the door. She was stopped in her tracks by another shower of stones.

RAT-A-TAT-A-TAT!

'Right. That's it! That's enough!' Gwenda yelled, as she yanked aside the blanket covering the doorway. 'I'm going to find out who's doing it.'

'Be careful, Gwen,' said Billy, but she wasn't afraid. She leapt up the steps from the shelter, just in time to see a gang of boys running out of the garden and along the side of the house.

The rest of us piled into the doorway and watched them legging it.

'I saw you, Ivor Ingrams,' Gwenda shouted. 'No good running away. I'm going to tell my father on you.'

Ivor turned. He was with his new evacuee friends. They'd all scarpered but Ivor came back up the path into the garden. He pointed his finger at us, huddled in the doorway and laughed.

'They getting you to fight their battles for them?' he jeered.

Quick as a flash, Freddo pushed his way through the rest of us and jumped up the steps to stand by Gwenda. He yelled back at Ivor: 'We can fight our own, butt, don' you worry. Anyway, we got one to finish off, haven't we?'

'Any time,' Ivor shouted back, but he turned to go. He didn't have anyone to help him, see, and there were four of us boys . . . and Gwenda. I wouldn't have liked to take her on – she was that angry.

'Clear off, you cheeky boy,' she shouted. 'Or I'll report you to my father.'

'It was only fun,' Ivor called back. 'Just wanted to give you a bit of a fright.'

Then he was gone, round the side of the house.

Gwenda raced up the path just to make sure.

'*Duw*, she's brave,' said Vic, watching her go.

'Or daft,' said Billy.

Truth is, we were all impressed. We'd never seen Gwenda like that before.

'We'd better be getting home,' said Freddo. He came down the steps and nudged his way back into the shelter. 'Come on, Al. Pack that puppet away in your bag, and let's go.'

He switched on the light so that Aldo could see what he was doing. The Pinocchio puppet was lying on the floor, all tangled up in its strings.

Very gently, Aldo started to pick it up. Then he gave a little moan.

'What's the matter, Al?' Freddo pushed past me to get a better look.

Aldo whispered. 'It's got broken, Fred. Look!'

He held out the puppet for us to see.

In the panic, when we'd all tried to duck for cover, one of the wooden legs had come loose. Worse than that, the nose had been snapped off. It was caught up in the web of strings.

'*Idiota*!' Freddo shouted, loud, making us all jump. 'You should never have brought it out of the house. It doesn't belong to you. It's Papa's. It's Papa's!'

Tears came quick to Aldo's eyes. He tried to tug the wooden nose free of the strings but his fingers were too big and clumsy.

Freddo grabbed the puppet from him and got hold of Aldo's bag. 'Give it here before you do any more damage.' He lifted the puppet into the bag.

The rest of us stood and watched, a bit shocked to see how angry Freddo was. Billy piped up: 'It was prob'ly my fault, Fred. When I fell on my side I might have broken it.'

Freddo stuffed the last of the strings into the bag and pointed at his brother. 'It wouldn't have happened at all if that stupid boy hadn't brought it with him.'

I'd never ever heard Freddo speak about his brother like that. He was always Al's biggest defender, his best butty. It just showed how things were getting to him. He slung the bag over his shoulder. One of the puppet's legs was pointing out of the top.

'They've gone.' Gwenda poked her head into the shelter, panting. 'The evacuees ran off down the street like the cowards they are. Ivor's cleared off too but I'll tell my father about him, don't you worry. My father says . . .' She stopped and pointed at Aldo. 'What's he crying about now?'

'Papa's puppet,' said Aldo. Tears were trickling down his red cheeks. 'I broke it.'

'Aye, and I just hope we can get it mended before Mamma finds out,' said Freddo, pushing him to the doorway. 'Otherwise you're in dead trouble.'

Chapter 9

Afterwards, we took the puppet back to my house and tried to fix it. We laid it out on the kitchen table just like in an operating theatre. We straightened out the arms and the legs and the head and the body. We untangled the strings.

I'd thought we could stick the broken nose back on with some glue from my dad's toolbox but when we'd opened up the bottle it had all dried hard.

My mam was at work, so only Nanna was in and she couldn't see what we were up to. 'What you doing, boys?' she asked, from her chair over by the sideboard.

'Making a model Spitfire, Nanna,' I said, a bit guilty.

'There's lovely,' said Nanna. 'I could do with nice cup of tea when you've finished.'

'Yes, Nanna.'

'Well, don't take too long, Robert.' She gave a little grunt. 'They're going to start rationing it soon.'

Then we looked for some wire to fix the broken leg, but we couldn't find any, anywhere. 'It's hopeless,' Freddo muttered under his breath. He gave the table leg an angry little kick. Nanna hadn't heard him because she was listening hard to the wireless. Lucky.

Aldo snuffled a bit. He'd stopped crying but you could tell he blamed himself for what had happened.

'We'd better try and smuggle it into the house,' Freddo whispered, 'and hope Mamma doesn't notice.'

So the broken puppet went back into its box and Freddo managed to get it hidden in the bottom of his clothes cupboard. Just for now. He said he'd try and buy some glue and fix the puppet himself.

That didn't stop Aldo from being sad, though. He wasn't his usual happy self at all. His mam thought it was because they still hadn't had any news about Mr Moretti.

*

'I know something that'll cheer you up, Al,' said Freddo one afternoon a few days later.

We were lazing around in the sunshine up on the hill above our village. School had finished because we were still only doing mornings.

Down below, the pit wheel turned and the noise of the coal trucks was carried up by the breeze as they clattered and clanged their way over the pithead tracks.

'What's gonna cheer me up, Fred?' Aldo propped himself up on one elbow and squinted at his brother in the sunlight. They seemed to be friends again. 'Shall we go and get Ivor and his butties? Bop them on the head?'

We'd sort of stayed clear of Ivor and his lot since the trouble up at Gwenda's. And they'd stayed clear of us too. Freddo had hissed at Ivor under his breath a couple of times in the playground, but they hadn't fought. Not so far.

'No, Al,' Freddo laughed. He jumped up and gave Aldo a hand to help him to his feet.

'What then, Fred?' I asked, glad that it didn't involve going after Ivor and his friends.

'Let's go and see Lizzie Morgan.'

'Who's she?' Aldo asked.

'A girl we met, Al. Me and Rob.'

'She lives over the hill at Tŷ Cornant farm,' I told him, getting to my feet too. 'They got animals.'

'She told us to visit, didn't she, Rob?' said Freddo.

'Aye, anytime,' I said. 'Coming, Al?'

Aldo dusted some ferns off his shirt. 'I like animals. 'What they got?'

'Dunno,' said Freddo. 'Let's go and find out.'

'YES!' Aldo yelled. And for the first time in days he gave us a big smile. 'Let's go and find out.'

Me and Freddo didn't really know how to get to Tŷ Cornant because we never usually played over that way. All we knew was that it was in the next valley to ours. So, we'd have to go over the top of the hillside.

We set off up the lane. It got steeper as we climbed, but the view got better. Ferns and gorse stretched as far we could see and, down below, our own valley snaked in between the hills. Black with coal dust, the river twisted its way along the valley bottom to the sea at Cardiff. The railway line ran beside it. Now and again there were villages, every one with a pit standing tall in the middle of all the houses. Sometimes there were slag heaps high above the villages. Big mounds of coal waste they were, dumped on the hillside by buckets carried up from the pits by wires stretched between giant pylons.

'Are we there yet?' Aldo asked every five minutes. But we weren't. We hadn't even got to the top of the lane.

Higher up there were one or two farms, and grey stone walls and scrappy little trees, bent over by the winds.

It was only when the lane ran out and gave way to thick, tufty grass that the next valley came into view.

'That might be Cefn Du,' said Freddo, coming to a stop and pointing. 'Lizzie's farm is near by there.' He wiped the sweat off his forehead. 'See, Al,' he said, setting off again. 'We *are* nearly there now.'

Aldo grunted. Puffed he was, and red in the face. 'Right-o,' he said, and plodded along behind his brother.

Freddo must have been kidding when he said we were nearly there because it took us ages before we found another lane leading down into the next valley. There were stone walls on both sides of the lane and you couldn't really see what was behind them. 'I'm going to jump up and have a look,' I said.

The walls were easy to climb but they were a bit dangerous because there was no cement holding the stones together. You could easily pull one of them down on yourself as you climbed up. Or so our mams said.

'I can see a big house,' I yelled, hanging onto the top of the wall. 'It's only a bit down the lane.'

It *was* a big house, too. Lots of windows and tall chimney stacks and a big front door. There were smaller buildings in the fields around it.

'What's that noise?' Aldo asked. He was sitting on the grass verge at the side of the lane.

Me and Freddo cocked our heads and listened.

It was the sound of an engine. Not a car. It sounded bigger than a car. It was coming from higher up.

Aldo got to his feet. 'Can you see anything, Rob?'

'No, Al,' I said.

Then suddenly I could. 'It's a tractor!' I shouted. 'Coming down here.' I scrambled off the wall. 'Let's go and meet it. The driver'll tell us where Lizzie lives.'

The tractor came into view. It was only the second one I'd ever seen. There weren't many round our way. It trundled slowly down the lane towards us, orange and heavy, and making a real din.

There was an old man in the driver's seat.

The three of us ran up the lane towards him, shouting and waving our arms. 'Scuse me, mister,' Freddo yelled.

'Scuse me,' Aldo echoed, panting a bit with the running.

The tractor took up nearly the whole width of the lane. And it looked like it wasn't going to stop.

The driver hadn't seen us!

We leapt up on the thin strips of grass at the edge of the lane and flattened ourselves against one of the walls. We were almost deafened by the noise from the heavy metal wheels. 'Oi, mister!' we shouted and waved our arms more wildly. 'Stop!! Slow down!'

At last the driver seemed to see us. He pulled on the brake and with a huge clanking and chugging, the tractor slowly came to a halt. The wheels towered above us, almost pinning us to the walls. The old man leaned out of the driving seat. 'What the hell you boys up to?' he shouted. 'You could have got yourselves killed.'

'Didn't you see us, mun?' I shouted back. 'We were waving like mad.'

'And yelling!' said Aldo. He got down carefully off the grass verge. Me and Freddo did too. We moved round to the front of the tractor to get a better view of the driver.

He was white-haired and thin, and he did look very

old. His glasses were as thick as pop-bottle bottoms. Perhaps he couldn't see very well, like my nanna.

'Do you know where Tŷ Cornant is?' Freddo asked, getting to the point.

'Aye. I do,' the old man said. 'That's where I'm going.'

Freddo whispered to me. 'Perhaps he's Lizzie's father.'

Aldo heard us. 'Are you Lizzie's father?' he called up.

The man laughed. '*Duw, Duw,* I'm old enough to be her grandfather.'

'Do you know her though?' Freddo asked.

'Aye. I work for her dad. On the farm. Is that where you're off to?'

'Yes,' I said. 'We're Lizzie's friends.'

'Oh well,' said the old man, laughing some more. 'If you're her friends, I'd better be nice to you, hadn't I? Do you want a lift?'

Chapter 10

So that's how we arrived at Tŷ Cornant farm, me and
Freddo and Al, with one foot each on the little platform
behind the driver, the three of us holding on tightly to the
back of his seat. We whooped and yelled with excitement,
but no one could hear us because the heavy metal wheels
made such a racket.

Turned out that the farm wasn't the big house I'd
noticed from the top of the wall.

A couple of army lorries were parked outside that one,
with soldiers coming and going up the front steps. They
were carrying boxes inside. Some of the soldiers waved as
we went past. We waved back and shouted, 'Hiya!'

Soon after that, the tractor turned off the lane and
trundled along to one of the smaller buildings that I'd
seen earlier. It was a house made of stone, with little
windows up and down and a slate roof.

Some chickens were pecking away at the cracks
between the cobbles in the yard by the front door. They
squawked off round the corner when we rattled closer.

A man came out of the house. He took a look at us
clinging onto the back of the tractor and he laughed.

He said something but we couldn't hear what it was.

Then the old man put the tractor's brake on and shut
down the engine, and the other man came over. He had a
round, sunburnt face and black hair. He wore an old shirt
with sleeves rolled up to the elbows. His trouser bottoms

were tucked into wellingtons. 'That's a fine crop of boys you got there, Idris,' he said, still laughing. 'Where've you been growing them?'

'Top Field,' said Idris, the driver. 'In the nettle bed.' He laughed too.

We did as well, a little, but we were a bit nervous, I think, waiting to see if we were welcome.

'They're friends of Elizabeth's,' Idris said.

'Are you sure?' said the man. 'They might be German spies for all we know. Parachuted down in the night!'

'I'm not German,' Aldo said, very indignant. 'I'm Italian.'

'*Welsh* Italian,' said Freddo, quick as a flash. 'Our Uncle Antony's in the RAF.'

The two men looked at each other, sharpish, but they didn't say anything to that, so I thought it was going to be all right. Now that Italy was in the war, I could never tell if people were going to be nasty to my friends.

'Lizzie!' the man from the house shouted, turning towards the door. 'You got visitors.' He turned back to us. 'Step down then, boys. Let's see if my daughter gives you the all-clear.'

'You Lizzie's father, then?' Freddo asked, hopping down from the tractor. He held up a hand to steady his brother as he edged himself off the little platform. I held onto Aldo's shoulders. As he got down, I followed.

'Who are they?' Lizzie came through the doorway. Her curly hair was tied up in a scarf wrapped round her head. She had blue dungarees on.

'Oh, it's you,' she said, when she saw us. 'The boys from the Glan.'

'Not enemy agents then?' said her dad, half serious, half smiling. Idris gave a little laugh and made the tractor seat wobble a bit.

'No, Daddy,' Lizzie said. 'I don't think they're enemy agents.' She was smiling too. 'Though I've only met them once.'

They seemed to get on really well. It made me a bit sad, to tell the truth. I wished my father was around for me to joke with.

'It's Robert, isn't it?' she said, looking straight at me.

'Yes.'

She turned to Freddo. 'And . . . um . . . Ed, is it . . . ?'

'No,' he said, a bit grumpy. 'Fred.'

'Sorry,' said Lizzie. 'Fred. I remember now.'

'Frederico it is, really,' Aldo piped up. 'But we call him Freddo.'

'You his brother, are you?' asked Lizzie. 'He told me all about you.'

Aldo blushed, fast as anything. 'Did he?'

'Yes,' said Lizzie. 'All good things. Don' you worry.'

She gave Freddo a wink that Aldo couldn't see. Now he was blushing too.

'You thirsty, boys?' Lizzie's father walked back towards the house. 'Could you do with a drink?'

'You bet,' said Aldo, padding along after him, heading for the door.

'Hang on a minute, Al,' said Freddo. 'You haven't been asked in yet.'

'You're all welcome,' said Lizzie's father. 'You coming too, Idris?'

'No, I'll get off home now, Mr Morgan,' said the old

man, climbing down slowly from the tractor. 'I'll be back first thing.'

'Aye, right you are,' said Lizzie's dad, waving us into the house. 'The baler's being delivered tomorrow, so we'll get started on the hay making.'

'Very good,' said Idris. 'Maybe these boys can come and give us a hand.'

'Now there's an idea,' said Mr Morgan and he followed us indoors.

Coming out of the bright sunny day, it took us all a while to see where we were. It was a big room, a kitchen, with a long wooden table down the middle and a big black iron fireplace at one end. The fire wasn't lit but there were little oven doors set on either side and a pile of logs banked up in a big basket close by. There was a paraffin lamp hanging from the ceiling.

'Have a seat, boys,' said Lizzie, walking through the kitchen to a little room at the back. The pantry, I guessed.

Each of us pulled out a chair from under the table. They made scraping noises on the stone floor.

'So, you're Al, then, are you?' Mr Morgan sat down next to Aldo.

'Yes. It's short for Aldo.'

'Right you are,' said Mr Morgan. 'My name's Gwyn. Short for Gwynfor.'

Lizzie came back into the kitchen with a big china jug. 'Pass us some mugs, will you?' she said. She set the jug down on the table. 'They're on the dresser behind you.'

Freddo swivelled round in his chair and took five mugs off one of the shelves. On the shelf above there were photos of a woman, smiling. That must have been Lizzie's mam.

'I'm going to give them some of Cousin Phil's elderflower cordial,' said Lizzie, pouring something from the jug. 'Is that all right, Daddy?'

'Lovely,' said Mr Morgan. 'That'll get them tipsy!'

Freddo and me looked at him, eyes wide. His face was deadly serious but then he gave a big laugh and rocked back in his chair. 'Don't worry, boys. You could feed this to a baby!'

So we sat and drank Cousin Phil's cool, tasty cordial and Mr Morgan and Lizzie told us all about Tŷ Cornant farm. It was called that after the big house we'd seen on the way.

Once it had belonged to the family that had lived in the big house. They'd all died a long time ago and the house had become a hospital for people who were getting over chest problems, and that's when Mr Morgan had taken over the farm.

He had five pigs and the chickens we'd seen in the yard.

Before the war he'd had a flock of sheep as well, but they took up too much land to feed off, so the sheep had been sent to market and now the farm grew more crops. Things like potatoes and wheat and barley.

Because most of the young men had gone off to fight or to work down the pit, Mr Morgan had to rely on old men like Idris to help him run the place. He was pleased that Lizzie had come home from London because now she could help too. And only last week, he'd been sent two land girls. They were women who had volunteered to work on farms. One of them was Lizzie's cousin Phil.

'We could always do with some extra hands though, boys,' said Mr Morgan. He pushed his chair back from the table and stood up. 'Specially this time of year. Harvest coming up, see.'

He drank down the last of his cordial. 'So, if you've got any free time, and your mams and dads don't mind . . .'

'Oh, yes please,' said Aldo. 'Papa's not home, but Mamma won't mind. Will she, Fred?'

'We'll have to ask her, Al,' said Freddo, a bit quietly. I think he knew that Mrs Moretti wasn't keen to let them wander too far away from home for too long. 'But if she says yes, it'd be great to come up here and help.'

'What about you, Robert?' This was Lizzie asking.

'My dad's away too, but I'll ask my mam.' As long as I was at home to feed my nanna when Mam worked late, I thought it would be all right.

'Well, mind you do ask,' said Mr Morgan, 'and if they give you the nod, you'll be very welcome. There'll be something to eat and drink too, if you come.'

'Aw, for definite, then!' Aldo rubbed his big tummy.

Mr Morgan laughed. 'A boy after my own heart. Likes his food!' He got up from the table and gave Lizzie a kiss on her forehead.

Freddo and me looked at each other, a bit embarrassed.

'I've got to go and help Phil with the milking, Liz,' said Mr Morgan. 'You got jobs to do as well, yes?'

That was the sign for us to go. So we got up too and shoved our chairs back under the table. We trooped out of the kitchen back into the daylight.

The sun was still strong, but it was beginning to sink over the hill above Tŷ Cornant. We'd better get a move on, I thought, or we wouldn't get home before blackout.

It was like Mr Morgan read my thoughts. 'Where

d'you live, boys? You're not going to be too late home, are you?' Then when we told him how far we had to go, he said, 'Better give them a lift to the top of the lane, Liz. That'll speed them up.'

So we climbed back on the little platform behind the driver's seat and held on tight as anything as Lizzie edged the tractor out of the yard and along the track to the lane. I was impressed, and a bit jealous, that Lizzie was allowed to drive the tractor.

'Cheerio, boys,' Mr Morgan shouted as we clanked away.

'Cheerio,' we shouted back. 'See you soon!'

Outside the big house, the soldiers were lying about in the back of the lorries. It looked like they'd finished lugging boxes for the day. One or two of them whistled at Lizzie, but she just laughed and steered the tractor into the lane. She was a good driver.

'What the soldiers doing there, Lizzie?' I leaned forward and shouted above the din. 'Is it still a hospital?'

Lizzie shook her head. 'No!' she yelled back.

'What's going on then?' Freddo shouted now.

'Can't tell you.'

'Why not?'

'Top secret.'

We were at the top of the lane. Lizzie brought the tractor to a stop. It kept on juddering away as we climbed off, me and Freddo helping Aldo down. 'Why can't you tell us what the soldiers are doing, Liz?' Freddo tried one last time. 'We won't say nothin'. Honest.'

Lizzie looked down at us, thinking. Then she said, 'Promise you won't tell.'

'Promise,' we all said at once, and Aldo added, 'Careless talk costs lives.'

'Right-o,' Lizzie said, and she leaned down from the driving seat. We closed in around her, though nobody could have heard what we were saying because of the noise from the engine and there was nobody up there to listen in anyway.

'They're getting it ready for German prisoners,' said Lizzie, eyes wide with the drama of it. 'Pilots, mostly, shot down by our ack-ack guns. The first ones are coming tomorrow.'

Chapter 11

'Where on earth have you been, Robert?'

My nanna was standing by the front door of our house. She must have heard us coming up the street, still gabbing away, excited by Lizzie's news.

'Just playing, Nanna,' I yelled. 'I forgot the time.'

Then, more quietly, to Fred and Aldo. 'Don' say no more about Tŷ Cornant. My nanna's got ears like a radar dish.'

'Who's that with you?' asked Nanna, cocking her head in our direction. 'Is it the Moretti boys?'

'Yes, Nanna.' We were almost at our front door now.

'Thank goodness,' said Nanna. 'We were worried sick. Your mam's out looking for you. With Mrs Moretti.'

'Oh heck,' Freddo whispered. 'Sounds like trouble!'

Aldo moved close to where she was standing. 'It's not blackout yet, Nanna.' He always called her Nanna.

'I know it isn't, boy. But your mam have had some news.'

Freddo went white as a sheet. 'Is it about Papa?'

'It is.'

Aldo gave a little moan and grabbed hold of Freddo's arm. 'Is he dead?' he asked, a sob choking its way into his throat.

'Bless you,' said Nanna and reached out like she wanted to take Aldo's hand. But because she couldn't see properly, she ended up stroking his elbow. 'It's good news,' she said. 'He's alive.'

Aldo yelled as big a yell as I've ever heard. Freddo did a little dance on the spot. I laughed out loud, my heart bumping away like mad.

Up the street, one or two heads popped out of their front doors to see what was going on. One of the women shouted, 'You having any trouble, Bessie?'

'No. No trouble,' Nanna shouted back. Out of the side of her mouth, she asked me, 'Who's that calling?'

'Mrs Corris, Nanna,' I said. 'Number 24.'

'Oh, there's kind,' said Nanna, and then she shouted up the street. 'Thank you, Mrs Corris.'

One by one the heads popped back in again.

'Where is he?' Freddo asked, calming down a bit. 'When's he coming home? How do they know he's alive?'

The questions came tumbling from his lips but Nanna just said, 'Shush now, there's a good boy. Your mam will tell you everything. You'd better go and find her.'

'Yes,' said Freddo. 'Come on, Al.'

He shot off up the street. Aldo followed. He took long, awkward steps as he ran. He kept shouting, 'My papa is alive. My papa is alive.'

'Can I go with them, Nanna?' I asked. I was on my way before she had time to answer. 'I'll come straight back,' I yelled.

'You better had,' said Nanna. 'I haven't had my supper yet, what with your mam going off looking for you.'

'Thanks, Nanna. I won't be long.'

I chased up the street after my friends. Freddo was nearly home by now, but I easily caught up with Aldo. Mrs Pritchard opened her door as we galloped past. Trust her, always on the lookout for gossip. 'What's happened, boys?' she asked. 'Bad news, is it?'

'My papa is alive!' Aldo stopped all of a sudden. I bumped into him from behind.

'Oh,' said Mrs Pritchard, looking like she'd bitten a lemon. 'There's nice for you.'

'It is,' said Aldo, and set off again up the street.

We got to the shop door just as my mother was coming out. Freddo had already gone inside.

'Where've you been till now, Robert?' Mam said and she grabbed hold of my arm as if to march me back off down the street. 'It's nearly blackout.'

'Sorry, Mam. Sorry.' I tried to wriggle free but my mother, small as she was, had a grip like a vice.

I was saved by Mrs Moretti. She came bustling to the shop door, smiling. I don't think I'd ever seen her look so pleased. She laid a hand on my mother's arm. 'Stay a bit longer, Myra. Share our happiness.' Then she burst into tears as she saw Aldo standing there, panting, sweaty, but smiling too.

He pushed past us to give his mother a big hug and, as he did, my mother let go my arm and said, 'Just a few minutes, then, Lena.'

We walked through the empty café and into the kitchen. Aunty Edda was there, chopsing away to Freddo in Italian, words tumbling out as fast as machine-gun fire. She got up from her chair when we came in and gave Aldo a big squeeze. She couldn't get her arms all the way round him, but she did what she could. Then she came over and gave me a squeeze too.

'Sit down, sit down,' said Mrs Moretti. 'Wherever you

can find a space.' She went over to the cupboard and fetched out a bottle of honey-coloured liquid and three little glasses. 'This deserves a celebration!' she said, filling each of the glasses to the brim. 'Frederico, there's some lemonade I've been saving for you. It's in the storeroom. Get it, will you?'

'Yes, Mamma.' He was off like a shot and back again just as quick with a big bottle of pop and glasses for us. Two treats in one day.

We raised our glasses, like we'd seen in the films.

'Chin-chin!' Mrs Moretti said and then we all sipped our drinks. My mother coughed as hers went down and Aldo had to pat her on the back. That made her cough even worse, so Mrs Moretti took over and patted her more gently.

'Must have gone down the wrong way,' said my mother, sniffling a bit, and trying to smile.

Us boys didn't have any trouble though. We emptied our glasses double quick and Freddo poured in some more. 'Tell us what you know then, Mamma,' he said. 'Tell us about Papa.'

'Well, the good news is he's alive. Uncle Dino too! They didn't go down with those other poor souls on the *Arandora Star*.' She made the sign of the cross on her chest.

Aunty Edda did as well and gave a little sob. She murmured something in Italian.

My mam nodded as if she understood.

Mrs Moretti took another sip of her drink. 'We finally heard from the shipping office in Cardiff.'

'Took long enough,' Aunty Edda grumbled.

'So when they coming home, Mamma?' Freddo asked.

The two women looked at each other, and then Mrs Moretti said, 'They're not. Not just yet, anyway.'

'Why?' Aldo wanted to know. 'Where are they?'

'They've been put on another ship,' Mrs Moretti said, with a little sigh. 'They're on their way to Australia.'

'*Terribile*!' Aunty Edda butted in.

Even I could understand that.

'After all they've been through. Torpedoed . . . nearly drowned, spending hours in that cold, cold sea.'

'Shh, Edda,' said Mrs Moretti sternly. 'At least they're still alive.'

My mam took a hanky from her cardigan sleeve when Mrs Moretti said this. Like me, she was thinking of my dad and wondering if *he* was still alive. She wiped the corner of her eye.

'Don't you worry, Myra,' said Mrs Moretti, noticing. 'Your good news will come too!'

Mam put on a sad little smile. I looked down at the table because my eyes were beginning to fill.

'Why Australia?' Freddo asked.

'It's the Dominions, Mamma, isn't it?' said Aldo, remembering what we'd told him. 'It belongs to the King.'

'Yes, it does. And they've said they'll take our men there,' said Mrs Moretti. 'They're building camps to put them in.'

'Prisoner of war camps?' said Aldo. 'Like the one up . . .'

He stopped because Freddo and me were staring at him, eyes wide.

'. . . up in England,' Freddo butted in.

'Yes,' said Aldo, a bit sheepish. 'Like that one.'

'I don't know what you boys are talking about,' said Mrs Moretti, shaking her head. 'Your father is not a prisoner of war. He's an internee. There's a difference. He hasn't done anything to harm this country. And when this war is over, he'll be back here where he belongs.'

'With his family,' said Aunty Edda, nodding. 'And everything he's worked hard for all these years.'

'By the way, have you boys seen Papa's Pinocchio puppet?' asked Mrs Moretti all of a sudden. 'I thought he'd packed it safe in our wardrobe but I can't find it.'

My heart skipped a beat. I swear I heard Freddo's and Aldo's do the same.

'N-n-no, Mamma,' Freddo stammered. He took a swig of his drink, so he wouldn't have to say any more.

Aldo shook his head, slowly, but the rest of him sat still as a statue, as if he'd been turned to stone.

'Oh well,' said Mrs Moretti. 'I expect I'll come across it soon. No hurry.' She began to gather up the glasses. 'We'd better do the blackout curtains.'

We all stood up then, us boys keen to change the subject.

Mam and me said goodnight and told them again how pleased we were to hear their good news.

As we walked home down the street we didn't talk, but my mam kept hold of my hand. She hardly ever did that, but I let her. I knew she was thinking of my dad. Like me.

Where was he? I wondered.

And would *we* ever get our share of good news?

Chapter 12

It was two days later when we got back to Tŷ Cornant.

Now that Mrs Moretti knew that her husband was alive, she spent all her time trying to find out more. She didn't get very far, Freddo said. It turned out that Mr Moretti and Uncle Dino had been put on a troop ship called the *Dunera*. It had sailed from Liverpool for Australia a few weeks earlier.

His dad and Uncle Dino were lucky, Freddo said, because only about 200 of the Italians were rescued from the *Arandora Star*. Over 400 of them had drowned.

'They were trapped on the lower decks,' Aunty Edda had told him, crying.

Because she was busy, Mrs Moretti seemed happy enough to let the boys out of her sight. And my mam and Nanna said they didn't mind where I got to, as long as I told them where I was going and I promised to be back well before blackout.

'And get my supper on the go,' said Nanna.

So, after school finished in the morning we headed for the farm. We knew our way now, so it didn't seem as far. To begin with, Aldo was a bit quiet.

'He's worried in case Mamma finds the broken puppet,' Freddo whispered.

But as soon as we got to the top of the hill above Tŷ Cornant, Aldo brightened up a bit. 'What do you think we'll be doing, Fred?' he asked. He started hopping his way down the lane like a big kid, wobbling a bit as he went. 'Will they let us feed the pigs?'

'Dunno, Al. By the sound of it, I think Mr Morgan needs help most with getting the hay in.'

'Can we ride on the tractor again?' Aldo asked, still hopping.

'Maybe,' I said, but I thought the tractor was going to be kept busy in the fields.

'Hope so, anyway,' said Aldo. He stopped hopping and walked down the lane in between us till we got to the farm gate. We could hear the tractor clanking away in the distance but we couldn't see it.

We passed by the big house. The same army lorry was parked outside, but there was no sign of the German prisoners. 'Perhaps they haven't come yet,' said Freddo.

'Or they've escaped,' suggested Aldo, half serious.

Two soldiers came out of the house. They were the ones we'd seen on the lorry the other day. Each of them had a rifle slung on a strap over his shoulder. 'Hiya, boys!' one of them shouted. 'Come courting again, have you?'

'That Lizzie's a bit old for you, in' she?' the other one said, joking.

'She's not too old for me,' said Aldo, puffing out his chest, and that set both of them off laughing.

We were almost at the farmhouse when this woman came out of one of the grey stone buildings at the far side of the yard. A shaggy black-and-white dog trotted along beside her. The woman was quite young, but older than Lizzie, I thought. She was dressed in corduroy trousers and a fawn shirt and she had a brown felt hat on her head. She saw us coming up the path and shouted, 'You the boys from Tregwyn?' She had the loudest voice I had ever heard. Like a foghorn it was.

The dog gave a little growl but she patted it on the head to calm it down and walked towards us in her brown boots. The dog was wagging its tail now. 'Are you,' she asked, 'Lizzie's friends from Tregwyn? The Italian boys?'

Freddo stiffened, waiting to see if an insult was going to come. 'I was born there,' he said, defiant sounding.

'And I'm Welsh,' I said.

'It wouldn't bother me if you were Martians,' said the woman. 'As long as you're ready to pitch in, you're welcome.' She stretched out one of her hands for us all to shake. 'I'm Lizzie's Cousin Phil.'

'That's a boy's name,' said Aldo.

Cousin Phil let out a great big laugh. She was very loud. Even when she was talking normally she was loud.

Freddo and me backed away a bit.

'My real name is Philippa,' she went on. 'So everyone calls me Phil for short.'

'You're the one who made the cordial,' said Aldo. 'That was . . . mmmm!'

Cousin Phil gave another of her big laughs. 'Liked it, did you?'

'Oh yes,' we said, hoping she'd offer us some more.

But all she said was, 'Well, it's thirsty work here, so maybe you'll get lucky later on. What's your names?'

We told her and then the dog waddled over and licked Aldo's hand.

'This is Captain,' said Cousin Phil. 'He's a sheepdog, but he's out of a job now that our sheep have all gone.'

'He's lovely,' said Aldo, stroking the dog's head. Captain licked his hand some more, tickling him, making him giggle.

Cousin Phil said, 'Are you going to help then? *Lend a hand on the land*, and all that. We're a bit short of workers, with harvest coming up.'

'What can we do?' Freddo asked.

'Well, Lizzie and the others are up in Top Field baling the hay, so you can help me down here. I need to muck out the sties and get the pigs fed. That all right with you?'

'You bet,' said Aldo. 'Where do we start?'

'Follow me!' barked Cousin Phil, and she marched back across the yard to the building she'd come from.

She pushed open the door and we followed her into darkness. It was smelly in there and hard to see. Something grunted. 'Nobody afraid of pigs, I hope?'

'No,' we said, but the truth was that none of us had been this close to pigs before.

'We've only got five,' said Cousin Phil. 'Come and take a look.'

It was getting easier to see now. Light came in from a tiny window and from gaps in the slate roof. The pigs were in a fenced-off pen in one corner. They were snuffling around on the dirt floor. They had pink-and-black skins, but one was nearly all white. She had a fat tummy.

'She's a bomper,' said Aldo. The dog stood by his side, staring at the pigs. His tail beat against Aldo's leg.

'She's having babies,' Cousin Phil said. 'Your first litter, isn't it, Snowy?' She patted the pig on the back. 'Now, who's going to get their feed ready?'

'Me!' said Aldo. 'I'll do that.'

The pigs grunted some more.

'Right you are,' said Cousin Phil. 'I'll show you what to do. And you two can come and clean out the chicken run and get their food ready.'

So that's what we did.

Aldo had to go in the kitchen and clean out the bins where the vegetable peelings and the few bits of left-over food had been put. Then he had to mash them all up into a kind of thick pudding for the pigs.

Me and Freddo had to clean up the chicken droppings in their little pen and then put down fresh straw. It wasn't hard work but it was hot and smelly. Now and again, the chickens would run in from the yard, clucking and squawking.

Cousin Phil said she was going to be busy in the field behind the farmhouse but she would come and check up on us now and again to see if we needed any help.

After a while, when we were getting a bit sweaty in the heat, she called out, 'Anyone fancy some cordial?'

'Oh, yes please,' said Aldo, and we joined in.

So, Cousin Phil told us to leave off what we were doing and come over to the farmhouse. There was an old wooden bench, all split and rotten, by the side of the front door, but that's where she told us to sit. It sagged a bit when Aldo sat down.

She brought out three big mugs of the pale, yellowish cordial and we sat and gulped it down in the hot sunshine. Captain lay across Aldo's big feet. Cousin Phil leaned against the door frame. 'You been doin' good work, boys,' she said. 'You can definitely come back. If you want to.'

We all said we did. 'I love it up here, aye,' said Aldo. 'It's special.'

'It is too,' I agreed.

'I don't want anyone else to know about it,' said Freddo.

'Aw, bless you,' she said and gave a chuckle. Even her chuckles were loud. Loud enough almost to cover the sound of the army lorry coming up the lane. It was only when Captain started whining that we looked up and saw it. Nearly in the yard it was. It came to a stop and Cousin Phil walked over to meet it.

There were two soldiers in the driving cab and two others sitting in the open back, rifles in their hands.

'This is them, is it?' Cousin Phil shouted.

Sitting in between the soldiers were three men in uniform. German air-force uniforms.

'Luftwaffe pilots,' Freddo whispered, excited. We stood up to get a better look.

The lorry door swung open and a soldier jumped out. 'Aye,' he said. 'First three. More tomorrow.'

The German pilots stared at us. They all looked very young. They were about the same age as Ronald Price's brother and he was twenty.

One of them had fair hair. The other two were brown-haired. They didn't look evil, or nasty or anything, just a bit fed up. Their dark-blue uniforms were dusty and torn.

We stared back.

The driver leaned out of his cab and said, 'Where'd you want them then?'

'You'll have to wait till Gwynfor comes down from the hay field,' Cousin Phil shouted back.

One of the soldiers in the back of the lorry put his hands over his ears and made a face.

'He should have been here by now,' Cousin Phil went on. 'He knows where he wants them to work.'

So the prisoners were going to work on the farm. That was exciting, and a bit scary, I thought.

The tractor came clanking into the yard, with Mr Morgan driving and Lizzie clinging on behind him. Captain shuffled to his feet and ran towards them, tail wagging.

'Sorry, Phil,' said Mr Morgan. 'Trouble with the baler. Got held up.' He brought the tractor to a stop and came across the yard. Lizzie followed, patting Captain on the head.

'Hello, boys,' said Mr Morgan. 'Still on the booze, I see.'

Lizzie and Cousin Phil laughed at that, and the soldier who'd put his hands over his ears when he'd heard her loud voice did it again.

'Do you need more help down here, Phil?' Mr Morgan asked. 'Have you finished pulling up the potatoes?'

Cousin Phil said she hadn't, so it was decided that the three prisoners could start work with her in the potato field at the back of the house.

The soldiers jumped down off the lorry and waved their rifles at the Germans to show that they should jump down too. They climbed down into the yard, a bit lost-looking.

We saw that they had the letter P painted on their trouser legs.

'Phil will tell you where to take them,' said Mr Morgan to the soldiers. 'Lead on, Phil.'

Cousin Phil went striding away. She shouted at the prisoners. 'Come on. Follow me. Follow me!'

One of them, the one with fair hair, said something to his mates and they started to shuffle off after her. The four soldiers followed.

Captain gave a little bark and padded up to the German pilots. The one with fair hair stopped and gave Captain a pat on the head and a little stroke. He spoke, very quietly, in his own language and Captain wagged his tail.

One of the soldiers nudged the man with his rifle and they moved on, out of the yard. The pilot who'd been speaking to Captain turned and gave us a bit of a smile as he went.

Aldo smiled back and gave a little wave.

'Al!' Freddo hissed. 'What d'you do that for?'

'He was nice to Captain,' said Aldo. 'That's why.'

Then Captain came over and gave Aldo's hand a lick and Mr Morgan said, 'You three had better have something to eat before you head off.'

He climbed back up in the tractor. 'What you got for them, Liz?'

'There's some lamb's-tail brawn,' said Lizzie as she went into the house. 'Will that do, boys?'

None of us had ever had lamb's-tail brawn but we knew it was something meaty and we didn't get much of that. So it was going to be a treat whatever it was.

'Aye, that'll do,' said Freddo, cheekily. 'If it's all you've got.'

Chapter 13

The brawn was lovely. It was bits of meat in a sort of jelly. Tasty! We had some more the next day when we went back to Tŷ Cornant. The day after that we had vegetable pancakes.

The school holidays had started and we could go up the farm every day from early in the morning. I would go and call for Fred and Aldo or they'd come to my house. This morning, I called for them.

Freddo came to the door of the shop. He looked sad.

'What's the matter, Fred?'

'We can't come out, Rob,' said Freddo, but he let me into the shop anyway.

I could hear someone crying in the back kitchen.

'It's Aldo,' said Freddo, leading the way through the empty café.

'Is he bad?'

'No. He's upset, that's all. Tell you why in a minute.'

He pushed open the door to the kitchen. Mrs Moretti wasn't there, but Aldo was. He was curled up on the big comfy sofa under the window. It looked like he'd been crying for quite a while because his eyes were all red.

'What's up, Al?' I asked. 'Why in't you coming out?'

'Don't want to,' said Aldo.

'Why not?'

He sat up as if he was going to tell me, but instead he started to cry some more.

'You tell him, Fred,' he snuffled. He took a crumpled-up hanky out of his pocket and dabbed his eyes, hard.

'The police were here before,' said Freddo, and, for a moment, I thought it was bad news about their dad.

'They took Mamma to the police station,' Freddo went on, a bit choked up. I thought he might burst into tears too. He didn't though. 'Gethin Richards came and took her away.'

'What for?' I asked.

'Just so they can keep an eye on us, I suppose,' said Freddo. 'Because we're Italians. Because we might be spies or enemy agents . . . or something stupid.'

He was more angry now than sad.

Aldo gave a big sob. 'They won't send her away, will they, Fred? Like Papa?' Tears rolled off his chin and plopped on the kitchen floor.

'No, Al, they won't. It's "just routine". That's what PC Richards said.'

That seemed to calm Aldo a bit but then something started him off again.

'And Mr Richards says they won't let us write to Papa.'

'Have he got to Australia then?' I asked. 'Have you found out where he's ended up?'

'No,' said Freddo, 'but even if we had, it'll be hard to write to him.'

'The Red Cross will help,' I said. The Red Cross was good at getting letters to men who'd been captured and put in prison camps abroad.

'That's it, though, innit?' said Freddo. 'Papa's not a prisoner of war.'

'He's an in-in–' Aldo looked at his brother.

'An internee,' said Freddo. Then, very sad, 'The Red Cross won't do much to get letters to *them*.'

'So we'll never find out where he is,' Aldo wailed, 'or . . . if he's well . . . or if he's bad. We'll never hear from him again. I know it!' He curled back up on the sofa, his big shoulders shaking. He had his back to us now, with his hands cupped over his head.

Freddo looked at me and raised his eyebrows. I didn't know what to say. We both felt a bit helpless.

Aldo mumbled something but we couldn't hear him properly.

'What you saying, Al?' Freddo asked.

Aldo rolled over on the sofa and looked at us. 'It's not fair,' he said. 'Papa hasn't done anything wrong.'

The front door banged shut. Footsteps echoed through the café. Aldo sat up straight and wiped his eyes again on his hanky. 'Mamma,' he called. 'Is that you?'

'It is,' said Mrs Moretti, and pushed open the door to the kitchen. Her happy look from a few days back had gone now. I think she was surprised to find me there.

'Oh, Robert,' she said. 'Come calling for these two, have you?'

I mumbled 'yes' and she sat down at the table.

Straight away, Freddo and Aldo got chairs out to sit beside her.

Questions tumbled out. 'What happened, Mamma?'

'What did PC Richards say?'

'Will they send you away?' That was Aldo.

Mrs Moretti smiled and patted his hand. 'No, sweet boy. Nothing like that.'

Then she told us that all the police had done was to

check her papers. And warn her that they might have to take away her wireless. Oh, and she wasn't allowed to go more than ten miles from home any more. 'So they can keep an eye on all my spying activities, I suppose.' She said this with a bit of a smile but her voice was angry.

Then she spoke quietly to Aldo in Italian, trying to make him feel better, I guess.

Whatever she said seemed to work. He gave one last sniff into his wet hanky and gave her a big smile.

'So,' said Mrs Moretti, getting up from the table, 'aren't you going up that farm?' She went to put the kettle on the big iron stove. 'They'll be wondering where you've got to.'

'Can we go, Mamma?' Freddo asked. 'Will you be OK?'

'I'll be fine. Don't worry. I got things to do.'

The boys got up from the table and we all said 'bye-bye' and headed for the front door. Aldo turned back as he was leaving. 'Mamma,' he called, 'did they say how we can get letters to Papa?'

Mrs Moretti came to the kitchen doorway. 'No they didn't. But don't fret. We'll find a way. When we know he's safe in Australia.'

She gave Freddo a look, almost as if she was expecting him to say something, but he didn't.

'Good,' said Aldo, satisfied for now. He added, over his tears, 'I want to write and tell him all about Captain and Lizzie and Mr Morgan. I'll tell him how hard we've been working. He'll be proud of us.'

Then Freddo pulled him out of the door and we ran up the street to the hillside and Tŷ Cornant.

Chapter 14

'Where you going?' Vic and Billy were hanging around on the corner of Bevan Street.

'Nowhere,' we shouted and kept on running. Not too fast, though, so Aldo didn't get left behind.

'Aw, come on, mun,' said Billy, catching up. 'You haven't played with us for ages.'

That was true. The last time we'd been anywhere after school with Vic and Billy was the day we went to Gwenda Lewis's air-raid shelter and Aldo had broken the Pinocchio puppet.

'What's the big secret?' Vic asked, running along by my side.

'Isn't one,' I said.

'We're just doing an errand for my mother,' said Freddo.

'She can't go far now,' panted Aldo. 'Police orders.'

We came to a stop. Freddo glared at his brother but Aldo didn't seem to notice. He was too busy getting his breath back.

'Don't believe you,' said Billy. 'You've made a den or something and you're not letting on.'

The truth was that we didn't want anyone else to know about working up at Tŷ Cornant. It was our special place, and we didn't want the others to come along and spoil it. Once one extra person knew, you could bet word would get out. Then Gwenda would know and, worst of all, so would Ivor Ingrams and his gang.

So Vic was right. It was a big secret.

'Got to go,' said Freddo. 'My mamma'll be waiting for us to get back.'

He set off up the street, almost pulling Aldo with him.

For a minute, it looked like Billy and Vic would follow, but they didn't. Instead, Billy shouted, 'We'll find out, don't you worry.'

And Vic added, 'We'll get Gwenda on your trail.'

They ran off down the hill, laughing, arms stretched out, weaving from side to side and being Spitfires.

We watched them go and then we carried on to Tŷ Cornant. Today was the last day of haymaking and Mr Morgan had promised we could help. 'Damn good harvest this year,' he'd told us. 'That'll keep a few mouths fed this winter.'

So we didn't go to the farmhouse. We went straight up to Top Field where we heard the tractor working.

There were more people there than I'd expected. Mr Morgan and Lizzie, of course, and another woman who must have been the land girl who'd come to work at Tŷ Cornant with Cousin Phil. We couldn't see Phil, and we couldn't hear her either so she must have been down at the farm. Old Idris was driving the tractor. Captain was running along behind.

There were more German prisoners too. The three men who we'd seen before and five new ones. They were all in their shabby blue uniforms. No jackets on today, though. Too hot.

The one with the fair hair waved at us when he saw us. Aldo waved back.

'What time do you call this?' said Mr Morgan, coming

across the field. 'Working half shifts, are you? Bet you've only come for the food.' He was laughing when he said it, so we knew he wasn't really angry with us.

'Come over here and I'll show you what to do.'

The hay had been cut a few days earlier and left to dry. Then it had been pressed into big cube-shaped bundles by a baling machine hooked onto the back of the tractor. Now, all the bales had to be loaded onto a cart and taken down to the barn for storing.

Our job was to help load the bales onto the cart. It was pulled by a big, shaggy-haired brown horse.

'His name's Saturn,' Lizzie told us. She gave him a pat but the horse went on chewing the strands of hay left on the ground.

'Roll your sleeves up then, boys, and follow what these men are doing.' Mr Morgan pointed to the prisoners, already hard at work lifting the bales onto the cart.

I didn't know why they didn't just run away. But, later on, I spotted the soldiers sitting on the army lorry at the far end of the field, rifles in their hands, guarding. There were more of them too.

It took the three of us to lift one of the bales, so we worked very slowly. As we worked, Idris drove up and down the field, finishing off the baling. Mr Morgan and Lizzie and the land girl followed, making sure the bales were all tightly packed and that there was no waste.

It was hard work and hot. Now and then Lizzie would leave off what she was doing and bring round a big pail of water and a wooden scoop. We'd lift the scoop up high and pour the cool water down our throats. Lovely!

After a while, my back started to ache and my arms and legs were scratched from the sharp stalks that poked out of the bales. Freddo and me began to slow down a bit, but Aldo just kept on going. Strong he was.

When the sun was at its highest, Mr Morgan shouted out for us to stop. 'I don't suppose you want something to eat, do you, boys?'

'I wouldn't mind,' said Aldo, wiping his forehead with the sleeve of his shirt. 'Depends what you got?'

Mr Morgan laughed. 'What we got, Liz?'

The tractor had stopped working now and everyone had just flopped down on the ground. The prisoners stretched out on the rough stubble and soaked in the sun.

'Bread and dripping,' said Lizzie, jumping up on the back of the tractor behind Idris. 'And chopped carrots, I think. I'll go down and let Phil know we're on our way.'

Idris turned the tractor on and they clanked out of the field.

'That do you, boys?' Mr Morgan asked.

It definitely would! We got up and began to follow the tractor down the hillside to the farmhouse.

'Want a lift?' The land girl caught up with us. She was leading Saturn by a little rope tied to his harness. 'You can hop up on the cart. I'm Bethan, by the way.'

There were hay bales piled high on the cart, but we struggled up on top of them and sat there like kings.

The German prisoners followed on behind with Mr Morgan. At the top of the field, the army lorry slowly got moving, keeping us all in its sights.

The prisoner with the fair hair came close up to the cart. Captain padded along at his heels. The man squinted up at us and laughed. 'You look such important people sitting up there.' He spoke good English. He had a kind enough face, I suppose.

'We are,' said Aldo. Freddo nudged him, but Aldo took no notice. 'It's our prize for being best workers, see.'

'Yes,' said the pilot. 'I can see.'

We bumped along for a bit, and then the German called up: 'What are your names?'

'I'm Aldo,' said Aldo, quite happy to talk. 'And this is my brother, Frederico. And this is our friend, Rob.'

'My name is Kristof,' said the man, smiling. He nodded his head. 'How do you do?'

Freddo and me grunted and turned away. I didn't want to talk to this man. He was our enemy, see. I think Fred must have felt the same because he whispered something to Aldo, trying to shut him up.

I heard Aldo whisper back: 'I was just being friendly. Nothing wrong with that, is there?'

'He's a Luftwaffe pilot, Al,' I said, whispering too. 'He comes to bomb people.'

The man must have picked up what I was saying. He looked straight at me and stopped smiling. He fell back a few steps to walk with the other prisoners.

'Hello, boys!' Cousin Phil's voice came booming out of the yard as we got near. 'I hear you've been working hard.'

'We have,' said Aldo.

'You deserve something to eat then,' she said and she waved us into the farmhouse. We jumped down off the cart and followed her in.

The land girl, Bethan, led Saturn into the barn, and then she came in too. So did Idris and Lizzie.

The prisoners had sat down by the bench at the side of the front door. They weren't welcome in the kitchen. Captain flopped down with them. The soldiers kept watch from the far side of the yard, over by the pig sty. They had their rifles with them.

'Tuck in then,' said Mr Morgan as we found ourselves a place at the table.

We did! It wasn't bread and dripping, like Lizzie said. That was just for starters.

Afterwards Cousin Phil brought in a vegetable pasty she'd cooked that morning. It was made out of carrots and onions and potatoes. It sort of oozed out over the serving dish because the pastry was all thin and broken.

'It looks like sick,' Aldo whispered. He was sitting right next to me but Mr Morgan heard him from across the table and gave a great big laugh.

'D'you hear that, Phil?' he said, rocking in his chair.

'What?' said Cousin Phil, getting ready to spoon out.

'The boy thinks it looks like vomit,' said Mr Morgan and gave another big laugh. Idris nearly choked on the last of his bread and dripping and some came out of his nose. Lizzie had to pat him on the back.

Cousin Phil pointed the spoon at Aldo, like a dagger. 'Does he now?' she said, loud as anything. 'Well, he'd better not have any then.'

She started dishing out the pasty. She was laughing. She served everyone else before she got to Aldo. 'Well . . . ?' she asked. 'Are you brave enough to try it?'

'Oh yes,' said Aldo quickly. 'And I didn't mean it. Honest.'

'Bet you did,' said Lizzie. 'It does look a bit evil, Phil.'

It did too, but it tasted lovely. The three of us wolfed it down, hoping for seconds, but Cousin Phil scraped up what was left in the big dish and took it to the prisoners.

'Sorry, boys,' said Mr Morgan as Cousin Phil and Lizzie carried out the plates. 'Got to feed our "visitors" . . .'

Idris sniffed when he heard the word 'visitors', and gave a little laugh to himself.

After that we had some malt loaf that Lizzie had made and we washed it all down with carrot pop.

'Lovely meal, girls,' said Mr Morgan. 'Thank you.'

'Thank you,' we all said.

'That was the best I've had for ages,' said Aldo, then he turned to Freddo and whispered something.

'Aldo needs to go to the lav,' said Freddo. 'Where is it?'

'In the corner of the yard,' said Mr Morgan. 'By the pig shed. You'll have to take a bucket of water with you to flush it.'

'I'll show him,' said Lizzie, getting up from her chair.

So Aldo went off to the lavatory and the rest of us helped to clear the table and take the dirty dishes through to the scullery behind the kitchen. We didn't have to help wash up, though, because Cousin Phil said there wasn't any hot water.

'We should be getting back to work,' said Mr Morgan. 'Want to get the last of the hay in. Come on, boys.'

We followed him into the yard.

The prisoners had finished their dinner. They had piled up their plates by the side of the front door. Captain was licking up the little bits of food that were left.

'Leave that, Captain,' said Mr Morgan and he pushed the dog's nose out of the top plate.

I looked for the prisoner called Kristof. He wasn't by the bench with the rest of them. He was sitting on the ground a bit further away, leaning back against the farmhouse wall. By his side sat Aldo.

The man was holding the knife he'd eaten his dinner with. It wasn't very sharp, but he was using it to chip away at a piece of wood. All the time he was talking to Aldo, showing him what he was doing.

Mr Morgan saw that me and Freddo were taking notice. '*Duw*, he's good with his hands, that one,' he said. 'Mend anything he will. Best odd-job man we've ever had.'

The man finished chipping at the wood and held it up to look at it better. It was shaped like a horse, sort of.

'Al!' Freddo shouted. 'Got to get back to work.'

Aldo and Kristof looked up. Kristof smiled and pushed the little horse down onto a pointed stick. He touched it with his finger and set it moving to and fro.

'He's made a little rocking horse,' Aldo called back.

'I don't care,' said Freddo, taking a few steps towards his brother. 'We got to go now.'

True enough. Idris started the tractor. Lizzie climbed up behind him. Bethan came out of the house and went to fetch Saturn from the cool barn where he'd been resting. Mr Morgan was already on his way out of the yard. So were the other prisoners and the soldiers.

Aldo began to struggle to his feet. 'Coming, Fred.'

Kristof put the little horse on the ground and gave Aldo a hand up.

Freddo shouted again, 'Come on, Al. You don't need no one to help you.'

'I'm comin', mun!' Aldo called back. Then he said

something to Kristof that made him laugh and he came shuffling across the yard.

Captain left off cleaning the dishes and padded over to lick his hand. Freddo and me started to walk up to the top field. Aldo trailed behind. 'That man is really clever,' he told us. 'He can mend things, Fred.'

'Maybe. But I don't want you talking to him,' said Freddo. He stopped and turned to face his brother. 'Right?'

But Aldo seemed not to hear. 'He said he could mend Papa's broken puppet. That'd be good, Fred, wouldn't it?'

'No,' said Freddo, a bit irritable-sounding. 'We don't need his help. He's not our friend, Al. He's our enemy.'

Bethan caught us up, leading Saturn and the cart. 'Hop on again, boys,' she said, 'if you want a lift.'

Freddo jumped on the cart, me following him. He bent over to pull Aldo on board. 'Don't have nothin' to do with him, OK?'

But Aldo kept on. 'He's nice, Fred. He's only carrying out his orders. He just wants to go home, that's all.'

'Bet my dad would like to come home too,' I said, giving Aldo a last heave up. 'And yours. Wherever they are.'

'Aye,' said Freddo. 'Rob's right.'

Aldo went quiet for a bit as we sat and swayed along in the warm sunshine. Then he said, 'Think how sad Mamma will be when she finds the puppet, though. If we let Kristof mend it, she'll never know it got broken. What do you say, Fred? That'd be worth it, wouldn't it?'

Chapter 15

That's what made Freddo change his mind really. He was still worried that his mam would find the broken puppet, and then he'd get the blame for letting Aldo take it out of the house in the first place.

He knew how upset she'd be. It was something special from when Mr Moretti had been a little boy and now it was damaged.

'She'll have forty fits,' Freddo told me. 'She's worried sick anyway,' – he caught his breath – 'not knowing where Papa is.'

I knew that feeling. We still hadn't heard anything about my dad. Every day we waited for some news, but it never came. Nothing, no letters, no word from the Admiralty, the people in charge of the Navy.

Sometimes I thought we'd never see him again. I know that my mam and my nanna felt that too because when I lay in bed at night, I'd hear them talking about it downstairs in the kitchen.

'Our boys have been pulled out of Narvik for weeks now,' my mother had said one time. I'd crept out of bed, quiet as anything, and sat in the dark at the top of the stairs, listening, hardly daring to breathe.

'God knows what's happened to him,' she went on and I heard her pouring herself another cup of tea.

'Well, at least he's not on any casualty list,' said Nanna.

'That's something to be grateful for. Pour a cup for me, Myra. Shame to let it go to waste.'

So, the morning after the haymaking, when I went to call for Freddo and Al at the shop, I wasn't really surprised when Fred met me at the door and told me they were going to take the puppet up to Tŷ Cornant. He didn't want to cause his mam any more aggravation, see.

Then he said, 'Grab hold of this, Rob.' He had a big roll of cloth in his hand.

'What's this for?'

'Mamma's decided she's going to open the shop again. She wants to put this up outside. To show we're loyal to the King.'

He unrolled the cloth. It was a flag, a Union Jack.

Mrs Moretti came to the door. 'Will you give us a hand, Robert?' she asked. 'Frederico said you would.'

'Yes,' I said. 'What do you want me to do?'

The plan was for me and Freddo to hang out of one of the upstairs windows and nail the flag to the top of the signboard that ran underneath. On the board it said, in big letters: MORETTI'S CAFÉ. Then, in smaller writing: MORNING COFFEE – ICES – REFRESHMENTS.

Mrs Moretti was going to stand across the street and tell us if we were putting it up straight.

'She doesn't trust Aldo to do it right,' said Freddo, as we made our way upstairs with the flag and some sharp tacks. 'So he'll be able to get the puppet out of the house while we're busy. Mamma hasn't said any more about it, but I'm afraid she'll go searching for it.'

'You're taking a risk,' I said, 'letting it out of the house.'

'I know,' said Freddo, 'and I'm not mad keen on that

Kristof seeing it either, but I'm worried for Al. It's for his sake. And mine, I suppose,' he added, with a bit of a smile. 'I don't want to be around when Mamma finds it broken.'

When we got to the top of the stairs, Aldo was standing there, licking the flap of an envelope. 'I been writing to Papa,' he said, and pressed down hard on the envelope to seal it up. 'I been telling him all good things about the farm . . . and how we're thinking about him all the time . . . And I wanted to know when he's coming home.'

I looked at Freddo. He knew what I was going to ask.

'No,' he said. 'We haven't had any more news.'

'But we will soon,' said Aldo. 'When the . . . *Dun* . . .'

He couldn't remember the name of his dad's ship.

'The *Dunera*,' said Freddo.

'When the *Dunera* gets there, we'll hear from Papa straight away, won't we, Fred?'

'Expect so, Al,' said Freddo, but he turned to me so that Aldo couldn't see him rolling his eyes. 'Come on, we'd better get started or Mamma will be wondering what's going on.'

Aldo put the envelope on the windowsill at the top of the stairs. In big writing it said: TO SIGNOR PIETRO MORETTI, AUSTRALIA.

'*Sig-nor*?' I turned to Freddo.

'Mister,' he said.

Aldo set off down the stairs. Over his shoulder was the big brown bag that he'd been carrying the puppet in the day it had got broken. 'The puppet's in here, Rob,' he whispered.

'I know, Al,' I said. 'I can see it.'

One of the arms was poking out of the top of the bag. Aldo laughed, quiet, and pushed it back in. He carried on down the stairs.

Freddo and me went through into one of the rooms at the front. I think it must have been where his mam and dad slept. There was a big wooden bed with a white cover and the room was filled with other pieces of dark wooden furniture. On the walls were lots of old photographs, a bit faded. On every one there was a group of men with moustaches, or men and women holding babies dressed in what looked like long white frocks. There were some pictures of a village on the side of a hill, with a big church tower standing high above the houses.

Freddo saw me looking. 'That's where Mamma and Papa came from,' he said. 'Before they lived in Wales.'

He pushed up the window and we both of us leaned out into the street.

Mrs Moretti was standing on the pavement opposite, arms folded. 'You've taken your time,' she shouted up.

'Sorry, Mamma,' Freddo shouted back. 'We were helping Aldo with his letter.'

We unrolled the flag so it hung down over the signboard and Mrs Moretti told us to move it this way and that till we got it all straight. I held it in place and Freddo tacked it to the wood.

There weren't many people around that morning, so there wasn't much to look at. Then I saw Aldo coming up the side street and turning the corner into Cardiff Road. He must have come from the yard at the back of the shop. I could see him but his mother couldn't. She was too busy making sure we were putting the flag up properly.

Aldo slipped out of sight, but not before he turned round and patted the bag that was slung over his shoulder. He saw me and Fred hanging out the window, raised a finger to his lips, gave a big wink and was gone.

'Is that all right, Mamma?' Freddo asked, giving a last bang with the hammer. Now he'd seen Aldo safely out of the house, he was keen to be going.

'It will do,' said Mrs Moretti.

'Right,' said Freddo. Then he whispered to me, 'Come on. Let's go before she asks where Aldo is.'

We shut the window, left the hammer and tacks on the floor and scooted downstairs and through the café. Mrs Moretti was coming in through the front door. 'Where's your brother?' she asked, but Freddo hardly paused.

'Dunno, Mamma. Maybe he's started off up the farm.' We were out of the door and into the street.

'Well, make the most of it!' Mrs Moretti shouted after us. 'I'll be needing some help here when I open the shop. You won't have time for playing farm boys then.'

'Yes, Mamma, I know,' Freddo yelled, as we legged it up Cardiff Road. 'See you later.'

Though there weren't many people around, there was the usual queue outside Jenkins the Butcher's. Because meat was rationed there wasn't much in the shops so, most days, there were lines of people waiting outside to see what was on sale.

A woman called out from the queue. 'Saw your brother going up the street, Frederico.' It was nosy Mrs Pritchard.

'You don't miss much, do you?' Freddo yelled back. 'You should be spying for Britain.'

Some of the other women nodded and laughed at that. 'Aye, that's true,' one said. A few of them turned to watch us as we passed by. When they did, Mrs Pritchard shuffled up the queue, trying to cheat her place.

No sign of Al yet, but then we turned up Watkin Street and saw him. He was surrounded by a crowd of boys, but standing taller than any of them. They yapped round him like a pack of noisy dogs.

'Damn. It's Ivor Ingrams,' said Freddo, and raced up the street, me following. 'What you doin'?' he shouted as we got nearer. 'Leave him alone.'

The boys turned to face us. Ivor pushed to the front. He had his usual bunch of cronies with him and Trevor Davies and Colin Vickers from our class. Billy and Vic were there too, looking sheepish now we'd turned up.

'Wasn't doing nothing,' Ivor smirked. 'Just wanted to see what he had in the bag, that's all.'

Aldo was clutching the bag tight to his side, the strap round his shoulder. He was half smiling, half worried-looking.

'Your butties by there said he had something special to show us,' Ivor went on, nodding at Billy and Vic.

'Didn't, Fred,' said Billy.

'Honest,' said Vic.

'Only said we'd seen him with the bag before,' Billy went on, all apologetic. 'Didn't say what was in it.'

'Must be special, though, if he's holding onto it so tight,' one of other boys said and gave the bag a little tug. Aldo held on even tighter.

'What's the big secret?' Ivor asked. 'What's he hiding?'

'Nothing,' said Freddo. He was getting angrier now,

I could tell. He still had a fight to finish off with Ivor and maybe this was the time to do it.

But he must have thought better of it because all he said was, 'Come on, Al. We got to get to Aunty Edda's.'

'Aunty Edda,' one of the boys said. 'Edda! What kind o' name is that, mate?'

'It's Italian,' said Aldo.

Freddo looked at him hard, wanting him to shut up. 'Come on, Al,' he said again. 'Don't let this lot stop you.'

Though there must have been about eight or nine boys ganging round him, Aldo was the biggest and strongest. It looked as if it would be easy for him just to walk away. But the others all started tugging at him harder now, pulling on the bag, trying to wrestle it from his shoulder. Billy and Vic stood back, watching, still a bit embarrassed.

'Leave him alone,' Freddo snarled. He pushed into the crowd, holding out his arm to pull Aldo free.

The boys whooped and shouted and grabbed at the bag even more.

Aldo had stopped smiling. He tried to edge his way through the crowd but the boys just packed in closer, laughing. Because he was hanging onto the bag so tightly, Aldo didn't have a free hand to shove them away.

Freddo launched himself into the scrum, tugging at the boys on the edge, me helping.

Then someone shouted, 'It's a dolly! He's got a big dolly!' The pushing and shoving stopped for a second.

Out of the top of the bag poked one of the puppet's wooden arms.

The boys screamed laughing. Aldo was close to crying.

Ivor jeered. 'Cissy! A big boy like you got a doll.'

'It's not a doll,' Freddo yelled, and he made another grab to pull Aldo free of the crowd.

'Looks like it,' said Trevor.

'Definitely,' said one of the others and, at that moment, Aldo reached out to take his brother's hand. That made him loosen his grip on the bag and, quick as a flash, it had been tugged off his shoulder.

'Got it,' the boy shouted and he threw the bag high into the air.

Aldo moaned out loud. 'Give it back,' he said. There were tears in his eyes. 'It's special.'

The bag came spinning down into the group, the puppet arm still poking out of the top.

Me and Freddo jumped up to try and grab it but Ivor got there before us and sent the bag flying again.

'It's yours, Trev,' he shouted and he broke free of the crowd and ran ahead up the street. Trevor jumped to catch the bag as it came down again and he broke free too.

'Your pass, Col!' he shouted and threw the bag to Colin Vickers. The others joined in now, running along the street.

'Pass it to me!' they shouted, leaping up and down in their excitement, arms waving. 'Over here, Col! To me! To me!'

I saw Billy and Vic slink away.

Freddo called after them: 'Cowards!'

Billy turned and said, 'We wasn't with them, Fred. We were only looking on.'

'Yeah, but you didn't do nothin' to stop them, did you? You're windy you are!'

They'd turned the corner into Cardiff Road by then and couldn't hear.

The bag was still being tossed around, the boys jumping for it, grabbing it, running with it. More and more of the puppet was breaking free.

'Come on out, dolly,' someone shouted. 'Don't be shy!'

They thought that was great. 'Don't be shy!' they yelled. 'Don't be shy!'

That's what made Aldo tamping mad. He gave a great big roar and went full pelt up the street after the pack. He wasn't crying now. He was like a wild animal. We charged along behind him as he pushed his way through the crowd, scattering the smaller boys as he went.

The bag was whirling through the air again and Aldo leapt for it. He was heavy, though, not quick enough, and Ivor jumped up and knocked the bag away from Aldo's outstretched arm. 'Got it!' Ivor shouted and the others screamed and jumped up and down.

Trevor and a couple of others went running ahead. 'To me, Ive!' Trevor shouted. 'Pass it 'ere!'

Ivor sent the bag flying up the street just as a man came out of one of the houses and stepped onto the pavement.

WALLOP! Straight into his chest.

'What the hell . . ?' he shouted and grabbed hold of the bag. 'What's going on here?'

It was Penry Lewis, Gwenda's father.

Ivor skidded to a stop, and shouted, 'Quick. Scarper. Get out of here.'

Mr Lewis stood on the doorstep, red-faced and panting. He still had the bag clutched to his chest. Two puppet arms poked up, like they were about to pick his nose. 'It's you again, is it, Ivor Ingrams? Gwenda's told me all about you throwing stones at my new shelter.' But he was wasting his breath. Ivor and his mates had all cleared off.

A man came out of the house and stood on the doorstep with Mr Lewis. It was one of his wardens. I'd seen him going round checking that everyone had their blackout curtains up. 'What is it, Penry?' he asked.

'A bunch of tearaways,' said Mr Lewis, and for the first time he seemed to notice the arms sticking out of the bag. 'What on earth's this?' he said, more to himself than anyone else.

Freddo stepped forward, a bit red-faced. 'It's ours, Mr Lewis. It's one of my toys from when I was little.' He took a quick glance at me and Aldo, hoping we wouldn't go into the full story.

'Italian, is it?' said the warden.

'Yes,' replied Freddo. 'It's a puppet.'

'Better not carry it around the streets then,' said Mr Lewis. 'Some people are a bit funny these days about anything to do with Italy.'

'Yes,' said Freddo. Nothing else. Though I bet he wanted to.

Aldo stepped forward, reaching out. 'May we have it back please?' His face was streaked with lines where he'd been crying. One of his shirt sleeves was ripped too.

'You may,' said Mr Lewis. He pushed the wooden arms back into the bag. 'But don't go carrying things like this around, upsetting people. Or you'll only have yourselves to blame if there's any trouble. Understand?'

97

Chapter 16

'He made it sound like it was our fault,' said Aldo.

We were in the yard at Tŷ Cornant and he was telling Kristof what had happened and why we were so late arriving. Everyone had finished eating their dinner, but Lizzie had promised us some bread and jam later on.

'It wasn't our fault, was it, Fred?' Aldo went on. He was sitting on the sagging little bench outside the farm door, side by side with Kristof. Captain was dozing at their feet.

The rest of the prisoners were at the far side of the yard, leaning over the gate to the pig sty. Snowy had had her litter the previous night, Cousin Phil said. Eight little piglets.

The soldiers were sitting in the back of their lorry, just watching.

No sign of Idris or the others. We guessed they were still up in the top field because we'd heard the tractor rumbling away when we legged it down the lane to the farm.

'No, it wasn't our fault, Al,' said Freddo.

'People don't think what they're saying sometimes,' said Kristof. 'Is that the puppet that is making so much trouble?' He held out his hand for the bag that Aldo was clutching tight in his lap.

Aldo'd been a bit teary on the way up but he was calmer now. The rip in his shirt sleeve wasn't too bad either. 'We'll tell Mamma you tore it on the brambles,' Freddo had said.

Aldo handed over the bag and Kristof undid the string that tied up the top. He reached inside.

Freddo and me were standing a few steps away from where they were sitting. We didn't want it to look like we were getting friendly with Kristof. Then, as he took the puppet out of the bag, ever so carefully, one of the arms tumbled free and fell towards the stone yard. It must have come loose in the rough and tumble with Ivor and his butties.

Freddo dashed forward and grabbed it. He handed it back to Kristof, and edged closer to see if any more damage had been done.

'Fred,' I whispered.

'What?'

'Don't get too pally, mun.' I sort of mumbled this because I didn't want Kristof to hear. He did though, I think, because he looked at me and gave a little smile.

'Will you be able to mend it?' Freddo asked him, a bit anxious.

Kristof untangled the strings of the puppet and lifted it up high. Now that it had been thrown around so much, it looked in a bad way. The broken leg was still snapped off, and the nose, and now it had a broken arm too.

'It's a Pinocchio,' he said.

'Yes,' said Freddo. 'It's my papa's from when he was little.'

'It's good, this story,' said Kristof. 'I read it to my . . . er . . .' He muttered something in German, and then said it louder to the men across the yard.

'Nieces,' one of them called back.

'I read it to my . . . nieces,' he said.

'Mr Morgan says you're good at fixing things,' said Aldo. 'You can mend it, can't you, Kristof?'

'Maybe,' he said.

'You'll try though, won't you?' Freddo edged in closer. Too close, I thought.

Kristof nodded. 'I will.' He jiggled the puppet up and down a bit to make it dance. It was all lopsided. He called out to the other prisoners again. When they saw what he was doing, they looked across the yard and laughed.

'Where's his nose?' Kristof asked.

'In the bag,' said Freddo. 'We tried to glue it back on but the glue was all dried up.' He moved forward to sit on the bench, next to Kristof.

He seemed to be getting a bit too friendly for my liking.

Freddo reached into the bag and found the long wooden nose. He handed it over, then Kristof held it on over his own, pretending it was his. He put on a silly voice and started singing some stupid song in German.

The other prisoners laughed some more, and so did some of the soldiers on guard in their lorry when they saw what he was doing.

Aldo and Freddo laughed too. I didn't.

'What's going on out there?' Cousin Phil's voice came echoing out of the farmhouse. 'Sounds like someone's having fun.'

Next thing, she was standing in the doorway with Lizzie peeking over her shoulder. They laughed when they saw what Kristof was doing, and that got him singing even louder. He made his pretend nose do a dance of its own up and down his arm. Captain raised his big head to look up.

'Punch-and-Judy man now, is it?' said Lizzie, laughing. 'Looks like there's nothing you can't do, mister.'

'Can't escape our ack-ack guns, can he, though?' I said, half under my breath. It was loud enough for Lizzie to hear. 'They brought him down, didn't they?'

'What's got into you, Robert Prosser?' she said. 'Don't you think it's funny?'

'No,' I said. 'I think it's stupid.'

Kristof stopped singing now and the others stopped laughing. Freddo and Aldo and Lizzie and Cousin Phil were all looking at me.

'It was a good laugh, Rob,' said Aldo. 'Kristof is funny.'

'I don't think so, Al,' I said. I wanted this talk to end now. 'I seen the infants do funnier things.'

Cousin Phil snorted, laughing, and turned back indoors. Lizzie turned away too, but she mouthed something at me before she went. I couldn't make out what she was saying.

I mouthed back. '*What?*'

Then she said it again and this time I made it out.

'*You're jealous*,' she said. She gave me a wink and was gone before I could say anything.

Kristof was folding the puppet into the bag.

'Don't stop,' said Aldo. 'It's funny.'

'Yeah, do some more, Kristof,' urged Freddo. 'It's a good laugh. Don't mind Robert.'

But Kristof said, 'No. This poor puppet is already not so well. Let us give him a rest.' He tied up the top of the bag and looked at me. 'I think Robert doesn't like me very much,' he said.

101

'I didn't say that.'

'No, but I think it's how you feel.'

'That's true,' Aldo chipped in.

'Leave it alone, Al,' I said, wanting to change the subject. 'Don't want to talk about it any more.'

Then Freddo said, 'Kristof's going to help us, Rob. Can't we all be friends for now?'

'Why, Fred?' I was beginning to get annoyed. 'Why should we be friends just because he's going to mend your blinkin' puppet? He's fighting a war against us. His lot want to kill us. For all I know they might have killed my dad.'

I don't know why I said that last bit, but I got carried away, and it just came out. I might have been right, though.

'We are only obeying orders, Robert,' said Kristof. 'I wish I didn't have to.'

'Don't then. You could have said no.'

We were both a bit angry by now, but we were keeping our voices down so the other prisoners and the guards wouldn't hear us.

Then Aldo said, 'Your papa's obeying orders too, Rob.' He turned to Kristof. 'He's fighting in our Navy.'

'And I think he would rather be doing something else,' said Kristof. 'Like me, I think he wishes he was at home . . . with his family.'

I could feel my eyes itching. 'Leave my dad out of this,' I mumbled. I know I'd started it, but now I didn't want to say anything else, because I thought my voice would start going shaky.

Lucky for me, Mr Morgan came out of the farmhouse

just then. He was wiping his mouth with a big blue hanky. Bethan was with him. 'Well, there's comfy you look, boys,' he said, seeing Aldo and Freddo sitting on the bench. 'Seems like I might have to send you all for an X-ray.'

'What for, Mr Morgan?' Aldo looked worried.

'To see if they can find any work left in you,' said Mr Morgan, keeping a straight face. Aldo didn't get the joke, but me and Fred looked at each other and laughed. That made me feel better.

Across the yard, the lorry started up. The prisoners were climbing into the back. Kristof stood up to join them. He patted the bag and I heard him say to Aldo, 'Leave it with me, yes? I will see what I can do to make it better.'

'Thank you,' said Aldo. So did Freddo. They got up from the bench and came over to where I was standing.

Kristof headed across the yard to the army lorry. The bag was tucked under his arm. He smiled at me as he passed. I didn't smile at him. Why should I? He was my enemy and my dad's enemy. I was glad he'd been shot down and kept prisoner.

Mr Morgan and Bethan were on their way to the barn. To fetch Saturn, I suppose. Captain got up, shook bits of straw from his fur and strolled along behind them.

The lorry drove off, noisy and smoky.

Mr Morgan called over his shoulder, 'Right then, you idle bunch. What you going to be doing this afternoon?' He stopped and told us that we could go up to Top Field to finish off the last of the baling. 'Or you can stay down here and help Phil.' He went on into the barn.

'Let's go up Top Field, Fred,' said Aldo. 'We can work with Kristof.' He shuffled off across the yard. 'Just going to the lav. I'll go and fill a bucket to flush it down.' I think Aldo liked going to the farm lavatory just for that reason.

When he'd gone, Freddo looked at me, a bit awkward. 'What do you think, Rob? Shall we go up Top Field?'

'I dunno,' I said.

Lizzie came out of the house, whistling, on her way to the barn. She must have heard us talking, because as she got to the barn door she stopped whistling for a second and looked at me across the yard. Her eyes were twinkling. '*Jealous*!' she mouthed, and went into the barn.

Freddo tried to coax me a bit. 'Come on, Rob. I can't let Al go up there on his own.'

'He won't be on his own, though, will he?' I said. 'He'll have his new friend to look after him.'

'Aw, don't be *twp*, Rob. Kristof isn't a friend. He's just doing us a bit of a favour, that's all.'

'Well, it looked like you were getting to be big friends. You were being real pally.'

'That was for Al's sake. To get Kristof to mend the puppet. That was all, mun.' Freddo gave me a little punch on the arm. 'Honest! You're my friend, in' you? Not him.'

'Stop gossiping, you boys!' Mr Morgan led Saturn into the yard. Bethan followed. 'Have you made up your mind what you want to do?'

'I'm going up the top field, Mr Morgan,' Aldo called out. He was on his way back from the lavatory doing up the *copish* buttons on his shorts.

104

'Very good,' said Mr Morgan. He and Bethan started to shackle Saturn to the cart. 'What about you two?'

Freddo looked at me, almost pleading. 'Come on, Rob. I've got to go with him. You come too.'

Lizzie came out of the barn to help her father finish getting Saturn in place. Bethan jumped up on the cart and took the reins. Lizzie jumped up too, still looking at me and smiling.

'Right,' said Mr Morgan. 'That's two down . . . one to go. Where you working, young Robert.'

I looked at Fred. 'Down here,' I said. 'I'm working down here.'

Chapter 17

All right then: like Lizzie said, I was a bit jealous. I own up.

So that's why I decided to show my friends that I didn't have to go along with everything they did. And I definitely didn't want to get pally with Kristof. Not for a hundred pounds!

I had a miserable afternoon though. I couldn't wait for Cousin Phil to say I could finish mucking out the pig sty. Oh aye, it was great to watch the tiny piglets with their eyes closed, snuffling around their mam, but I wanted Fred and Al to be there to see them too.

So I was glad when Cousin Phil shouted, 'That's enough for today, Robert. You can hop off and find your pals now.'

'Right-o!' I said, on the run almost as soon as she'd finished speaking. I couldn't wait to get to the top field and make it up with Freddo.

'See you tomorrow?' Phil boomed.

'Maybe,' I called back. Secretly, I thought that it would be good to spend a few days away from the farm, just me and my butties.

'Suit yourself,' she laughed, but I was out of the yard by then and legging it up the lane.

Halfway up, I heard the army lorry bumping its way down from the top field. In a bit, it came into view. The German prisoners were all sitting on the back with the soldiers. They were taking them back to their camp in the big house.

I stopped running and squeezed up against the stone wall to let the lorry pass. 'Looks like you're in a hurry, boyo,' one of the soldiers said, leaning out. 'Got a date, have you?'

'It's that Lizzie,' said another. 'Told you before, young man. She's too old for you.'

I stuck my tongue out at them and they laughed. The lorry edged on by.

Kristof waved at me, but I didn't wave back. No longer pinned up against the wall, I was on the move again.

The gate to the top field was wide open. Work seemed to have stopped for the day. Mr Morgan and Idris were checking some of the bales on Saturn's cart and Bethan was giving him a drink from a big tin bucket. Lizzie was lying on her back in the stubbly grass, soaking up the sun.

There was no sign of Freddo and Aldo.

Mr Morgan saw me standing by the gate. 'Escaped Phil's clutches have you, Robert? *Duw*, you're lucky!'

Idris gave a little chuckle.

Lizzie sat up and shielded her eyes against the sun to look at me. 'You're too late,' she said. 'Your friends have gone.'

'Gone where?'

'Buckingham Palace.' She scrambled to her feet. Her curly hair came loose from the scarf thing she wore round the top of her head. She pushed it back in place and walked over. 'Gone home, of course.' She kicked up dust and bits of straw as she walked. 'Where'd you think?'

'Why didn't they wait for me?'

'Perhaps they thought you wouldn't want them to.'

I turned away and headed on up the lane. I was angry again now, and more disappointed than I wanted to let on.

They couldn't even be bothered to wait for me. Some friends!

Lizzie called after me, 'You're not surprised, are you? Not after the way you were behaving.'

I stormed off, shouting back, 'Dunno what you mean.'

'Yes, you do,' Lizzie yelled. 'You're acting like a baby.' She started running to catch up with me, but I ran too, faster than her. 'They're your good friends, Robert. They're not going to stop being your friends just because of Kristof.'

I was almost out of earshot now, so when I could hardly hear her any more, I stopped running and turned round to see what she was doing. She was standing in the lane, panting a bit. She waved and shouted at the top of her voice, 'See you tomorrow!'

'Don't bank on it,' I yelled back, and turned for home.

I was in a bad, bad mood.

All right, Fred and Aldo didn't know I'd planned to go and meet them, but they could have hung around, couldn't they? Just in case.

I kicked out at every loose stone in the lane and picked up a stick to use as a bayonet. I didn't know who my target was. Sometimes it was Fred, but mainly it was Kristof. It was all his fault.

That's what kept me going for my long walk home by myself.

I was nearly on the edge of our village, where the lane

dropped down from the hillside to the first of the houses, when I heard the planes.

At first there was just a low droning noise, like a giant swarm of bees.

I swivelled round and squinted up at the sky. Behind me, high up, was a black cloud. German bombers flying close together.

Heinkels they were. Two-propeller jobs.

I could recognise them from the spotter cards we'd been collecting in the newspapers.

They didn't screech like the Stuka that had fired on us a few weeks back. Their engines made a tinny, stuttering sound . . . zzooorzh . . . zzoooorzh . . . they went . . . pumph-er pumph-er.

I could count them against the clear sky. Eighteen . . . nineteen . . . twenty . . . all heading across the valleys to the coast. To the docks, I thought, or the ammunition factory, or the airfield where Freddo's Uncle Antony was a pilot in the RAF.

From far off came the noise of an air-raid siren sounding a warning. You could only just hear it above the din of the roaring planes. By now, they were directly overhead.

I clamped my hands to my ears and stood rooted to the spot watching them pass.

These were part of Kristof's lot, I thought.

They flew on. The noise died away a bit.

Soon they were little black spots in the distance, no bigger than bees.

Then, BOOMPH!

One of the planes had found a target.

Far away, a cloud of smoke swirled up as the first of the bombs smashed into the ground.

I could see and hear it as clear as anything from where I was standing.

And now our anti-aircraft guns started up. They made a huge racket, drowning out the distant noise of the plane engines. I didn't see any take a hit, though.

BOOMPH! Another explosion, then another but, soon after, the planes flew out of sight and I couldn't see or hear what was happening any more. The ack-ack guns died away.

My heart was pounding. I wanted to get home. And, most of all, I wanted to get back to Fred and Al and tell them what I'd seen.

'Jiminy Cricket!' A voice came out of the quiet behind me. 'Did you see that?'

I knew who it was. Billy Harris. With Vic, of course.

'That was corking!' said Vic.

They were poking their heads over the stone wall at the side of the lane.

'Did you see it, Rob?' asked Billy. 'There must have been at least fifteen of them.'

'Twenty,' I said. 'What you doing there?'

'Nothing much,' said Vic.

'We saw Fred and Al come by earlier on,' said Billy. He began to climb over the wall. 'They were on their way home.'

'I'm surprised you showed your face to them,' I said. 'After what happened with Ivor and his gang.'

'We told you, Rob. We weren't with them. We were just looking. Honest.'

'Oh yeah,' I said. 'Looking *and laughing*. I saw you.'

Billy tried to change the subject. 'We wondered why you wasn't with Fred and Aldo. Not like you to split up.'

Vic pulled himself up on top of the wall. 'Aldo said you had a bit of a row.'

'Did he? He was lying.' I started walking on down the lane.

Billy called after me. 'He said he didn't know if you were friends any more.'

That stopped me.

'You can come and play with us if you like,' said Billy. 'We're going over the Pandy tomorrow.'

I turned to look at them. 'Can't. My mam won't let me go over there.'

'Well, all right, you could take us where you've been playing.'

'Tŷ Cornant?' I said, before I could stop myself. I didn't want anyone else coming to our special place. Well, what *had* been our special place.

'Where's Tŷ Cornant then?' Vic asked.

'A long way from here,' I said and I walked on home.

Chapter 18

'You're spending too much time up at that farm,' Nanna grumbled when I got in. She switched off her wireless. 'I was worried sick when I heard those bombers going over.'

'I saw them, Nan,' I told her. I opened the oven door and struck a match to light the gas. We were having some sort of stew for supper and I had to get it heated up for when Mam came home. 'They were heading Swansea way, those Heinkels.'

'*Duw, Duw*,' said Nanna. 'There's trouble for someone.' And straight after, 'See if there's a little something to eat in the pantry, there's a good boy. I'm starving hungry.'

'It's going to be supper-time soon, Nanna,' I said. I closed the oven door and blew out the match. I watched the tiny trail of smoke curling up to the ceiling. 'Anyway, I might not be going up the farm any more.'

'Why's that?' she said. She slipped a hand into the pocket of her apron, grumbling to herself.

'They've finished the harvest early.'

Nanna took something out of the apron pocket and slipped it in her mouth. A cough sweet, it smelled like. Sometimes I thought that because she couldn't see *us* very well she forgot that we could see *her*. 'What you eating, Nanna?'

'Just something for my cough, boy,' she said.

'You haven't got a cough, Nanna.'

112

'No! But this will stop me from getting one, won't it?'

She sucked away at the sweet, happier now. Eat anything, my nanna would.

Then she remembered something. 'A letter came this morning after you and Myra had gone out. It's on the mantelpiece.'

There was a brown envelope on the shelf above the empty fireplace. It was tucked in behind a picture of my dad in uniform just after he'd joined the Navy.

I reached up to get the envelope.

'Who's it to?' Nanna asked.

'Mam,' I said.

My voice trembled a little bit because I could see who had sent it.

'Does it say where it's from?' Nanna asked.

'Yes.' I calmed my voice down. 'It's from the Admiralty.'

'Oh dear, dear, dear,' Nanna went. 'Your mam wrote to them again to see if they got any news of your father.'

'Yes.'

'Open it, Robert. See what it says.'

'I can't, Nanna. It's not addressed to me.'

'Oh, give it here, then, and I'll open it.'

'We ought to wait, Nanna.' Part of me was as keen as she was to find out what the letter said. But part of me wasn't, the part that was frightened of bad news. Then I remembered. If it was really bad news, if someone had been killed, then the Admiralty usually sent a telegram, so this might mean . . .

There was a knock at the front door. I stood there with the envelope in my hand, not knowing what to do.

'Oh drat, there's a nuisance,' said Nanna.

Another knock.

'Better see who it is, Robert.'

I put the letter on the kitchen table and walked through the passage to the front door. There were voices outside, talking quiet. Too quiet for me to recognise who it was or what they were saying.

I opened the door.

'Hiya, Rob.' It was Freddo.

And Aldo. 'How be, Rob?'

'Hello,' I said, not very friendly though.

Freddo carried on. 'We came to see if you're all right.'

'Bit late, in' it?' I said. 'If you'd waited for me to come home with you, you could have found out then.'

'We thought you were angry with us.'

'Because of Kristof,' said Aldo.

Nanna shouted from the kitchen. 'Who is it, Robert? Who's there?'

'Just boys from school, Nanna.'

Freddo looked at me, a bit shocked. He said, quiet, so Nanna wouldn't hear. 'We're your friends, Rob. Not just "boys from school".'

Then Aldo called out, making sure she could hear. 'It's us, Nanna. It's Aldo and Frederico.'

'Well, tell them to come in, Robert. They can hear our news.'

'What news is that?' Freddo asked.

'We've had a letter from the Admiralty,' I said. 'I expect it's about my dad.'

Nanna called out again. 'Are you coming in, boys?'

Freddo looked at me as if to say, well, are we?

'They don't want to, Nanna,' I said. 'They haven't got time now.'

I didn't know why I was behaving like this. I suppose I still wanted to pay them back for making friends with someone I didn't like. And, now, for coming home without me.

'Oh, right-o,' said Nanna. 'Tell them you'll see them tomorrow then.'

'I'll see you tomorrow,' I said, going to close the door.

'Hope so,' said Freddo. 'Then we can be butties again.'

I grunted, because I didn't want to say 'yes' or 'no'.

Deep down, though, I did want to get back to being friends. For definite. When I could find the best way to do it.

'See you then, Rob,' said Aldo, turning away, a bit sad.

'See you,' I said, going to close the door.

Freddo put his hand on it to stop me. 'I hope the letter is good news,' he said.

'Right.' I closed the door. I stood in the passage and listened to them talking as they went up the street.

I was ashamed of how I'd behaved, but I also felt a bit hopeful that everything could be all right again. Somehow.

'Where are you, Robert?' Nanna called. 'What you doing?'

'I'm coming, Nanna.'

I walked through to the kitchen. Nanna was sitting at the table, holding the brown envelope in her hand. I think she'd been trying to open it, but she hadn't managed to. She waved it towards me. 'Do it for me, boy.'

'I don't want to, Nanna. I'm scared.'

'Of your mother? Don't be. I'll take the blame.'

'No, I'm not scared of Mam.' Though I was. 'I'm scared of what it'll say.'

'Well, sooner or later, we're going to find out, so open it now and read it to me.'

I sat down and picked up the envelope. I started to run my finger under the top edge where it was fastened down. I was trembling again.

SLAM! went the front door.

'It's me!' called my mother.

I put the envelope on the table, fast, like a thief caught on the job. I turned it address side up and smoothed it down flat.

'I hope the oven's on,' my mother called. 'I'm starving.'

Then, as she came into the kitchen, tired-looking as ever, she said, 'They bombed the munition works today.'

'Oh, there's terrible,' said Nanna, nearly choking on the last of her cough sweet. 'I hope Phyllis Bevan's all right.'

'They didn't get any of the buildings,' said Mam. 'Just the main gate, so the talk goes . . .'

She stopped. 'What are you two up to? You look as guilty as sin.'

Then she saw the envelope. 'Oh!' she said.

She sat down at the table next to Nanna. 'When did this come?'

'This morning, Myra. After you'd gone to the factory.'

My mother had torn open the envelope and taken out the letter inside. She unfolded it and began to read. The thin, crinkly paper trembled a bit in her hands.

116

Her lips moved as she read on but she didn't say the words out loud.

Then she began to cry very quietly. A tear rolled down her cheek. She brushed it away.

I put my hand on her shoulder and she patted it. I wanted to cry too.

'What is it, My?' Nanna asked. Her voice was all choked-up and scared-sounding. 'What can they tell us?'

'Nothing!' said Mam. 'They can't tell us a thing.' She gave a big sniff and wiped her eyes. She wasn't crying any more. Now she was beginning to sound angry. 'It's just the usual stuff,' she said. 'They're not able to tell us where he is because they don't know themselves.'

She read a bit to us. *It would be most helpful if you were able to provide us with the name of the ship on which Mr Prosser is currently serving . . .*

She slammed the letter down on the table. 'Well, we don't damn well know, do we!' she said, still angry. 'That's the point!'

Last time Dad wrote, months back, he said he was going to be transferred to another ship but he didn't know which one.

She picked up the letter again and read a bit more. *I hope you will take some comfort from the fact that Mr Prosser's name has not appeared on any casualty lists of those ships lost in action . . .*

'That's good,' said Nanna. 'See . . . like I keep telling you, Myra. No news is good news.'

'Oh, Mam!' My mother pushed her chair back and went to light the gas under the kettle. 'It's not enough!'

117

She banged the kettle down on the stove. 'I'm wondering all the time where Tom is. If he's well . . . if he's ever going to come home.' She lifted cups off the shelf. Now she was getting in a real state. 'I'm tired of writing letter after letter and not knowing if they'll find him.'

She plonked the cups down on the table and started crying again. Big tears this time.

'Now, now,' said Nanna, reaching out a hand to where she thought my mother was standing. 'Don't go upsetting yourself, My.'

I just sat there, not knowing what to do. I didn't like seeing my mam like this.

'I've had it up to here,' she said, touching her forehead. She sat down again and scrunched up the Admiralty letter in one hand. 'Worried sick I am.'

She sniffed again, stopped her crying. 'Sorry, Robert,' she said. She tried to give me a little smile.

'That's all right, Mam,' I said, but really and truly I didn't want to be there. I wanted to be with my friends.

'Mam,' I said. 'Can I just go and see Freddo and Al? There's something I forgot to tell them.'

Mam nodded. 'Don't be long, though, there's a good boy.' She patted me on the head but I was out of the house and up the street in a flash.

I didn't really have anything I wanted to tell Freddo and Al.

I just wanted to be away from the grown-ups and all their worries.

Chapter 19

The Morettis' front door was closed, but I banged on the glass and waited.

Mrs Moretti called out from far inside the shadowy café. 'Who is it?'

I couldn't blame her for being careful. They'd had their windows smashed in and things had been stolen.

'It's only me: Robert.'

'Oh, Robert.' The voice came nearer. 'The boys told me your mother had got a letter.' She was behind the door now, putting the key in the lock. 'We were all worried for you.'

I felt a bit guilty for a second, but then Mrs Moretti unbolted the door and almost pulled me inside.

'It's not bad news, I hope.'

'No . . . not really,' I said, and before I could say anything else, she pulled me towards her and gave me a big hug. She smelt of scent and warm bread.

'Thank God,' she sighed. Then she let go of me and locked the door again. 'Come and tell the boys.'

She led the way into the kitchen.

Freddo was on the couch, reading. Aldo was sitting at the table, finishing off his supper. He was twisting a pile of spaghetti onto his fork, but he stopped when he saw me. 'Rob,' he said. 'What's happened?'

Freddo looked up from his book. 'What you doing here, then?' He didn't sound very friendly.

'I come to tell you about the letter,' I said, a bit sheepish.

'Oh,' said Freddo. And he went on reading.

'Frederico,' said his mother, very sharp. 'Don't be so rude.' She went over and took the book from him. He glared at her but didn't say anything.

Then he looked at me. 'What did the letter say then? Is your dad all right?'

'Think so,' I said. 'But they don't know where he is.'

'Just like Papa,' Aldo said and shovelled the spaghetti into his mouth. He didn't seem to be angry with me. Freddo was, though. Couldn't blame him really.

Mrs Moretti started to clear the plates off the table. 'Tell your mamma not to give up hope, Robert. Tell her she's in my prayers.'

'I will,' I said. Then I didn't know what else to say. So, I mumbled something about how I'd better be going.

But Aldo had been thinking about his father. 'When Papa gets to Australia,' he said, licking the pasta sauce from his lips, 'what will they do to him?'

Mrs Moretti put down the plates she was carrying and sat beside him at the table. 'They will put him in a camp and look after him,' she said, glancing at Freddo.

He looked back, not reacting.

Then, just to make sure that Aldo understood, she said gently, 'Your papa will probably be there until this war ends. But I am sure he will be treated like the decent man he is. We must stay strong for him. And one day we will all be together again.'

Tears came to Aldo's eyes. 'I want him to come home.'

'He can't, Al,' said Freddo. 'Not yet. But he will one day, won't he, Mamma?'

'Yes. One day.'

Aldo sniffed. 'As soon as we know where he is, I can send my letter.'

'Australia's a big place, Al,' said Freddo, looking at me. 'Innit, Rob?'

'Yes,' I said, pleased that Freddo had brought me into the conversation.

He went on, 'We'll have to wait till we hear the name of Papa's camp.'

'Don't want to wait,' said Aldo, a bit sulky. 'I want him to know we're all right.'

'We'll see what we can find out,' Mrs Moretti said and she shook her head at Freddo. I think she was warning him to stay off the subject. 'Let's see him safely off that boat first.'

When she mentioned the *Dunera,* Aldo got even more tearful. 'When will it get there, Mamma?'

'Soon,' she said, patting his hand.

'How soon?'

Mrs Moretti looked to Freddo for help.

'It can take . . . oh . . . weeks to get to Australia, Al,' said Freddo. 'So there can't be long to go now.'

'And then we'll know where he's going to be settled,' said Mrs Moretti, giving his hand another pat.

But this didn't make Aldo feel any better. 'I miss Papa,' he moaned. 'I want him here. With us.'

Mrs Moretti stopped him. 'I've got an idea,' she said, pushing her chair back from the table and standing up. 'What if we all have a good look for Papa's Pinocchio puppet and keep it down here in the kitchen . . . to remind us of him.'

Aldo blinked the tears away. His eyes went wide as saucepan lids.

Freddo turned white.

I stared down at my feet. My breathing had gone a bit funny.

'I still can't think where it's got to,' said Mrs Moretti. 'It's not in your room, is it, boys?'

'No, Mamma,' said Freddo with a bit of a catch in his throat. 'It's definitely not in our room.'

He got up and gave a great big yawn. 'Can we look for it tomorrow? I'm tired, aye.'

He yawned again. So did Aldo, a loud, exaggerated yawn.

'Oh . . . right . . .' said Mrs Moretti. But she did look at them strangely. I think she knew something was up. 'But let's make sure we do, yes? Tomorrow.' She stroked Aldo's hair. 'Perhaps it will help bring Papa a little closer to home.' She smiled at the boys.

They smiled back, a bit sickly, then Mrs Moretti gathered up the plates from the table and took them over to the bosh to rinse them.

'I better be off now,' I said, relieved to be able to go. 'It'll be blackout soon.'

'Yes,' said Mrs Moretti. 'But you tell your mother we're thinking of her.'

'I will.' I headed for the kitchen door.

'Comin' up the farm tomorrow, then, Rob?'

I didn't hesitate. It looked like I still had my friends.

'You bet, Freddo,' I said.

Chapter 20

'Made up, have you?' asked Lizzie.

We were sitting on the bench by the front door of Tŷ Cornant when she came out of the kitchen.

'Nothing to make up,' said Freddo.

'Oh right.' Lizzie laughed and leaned against the door post. She turned her head to look straight at me.

I started to blush, I think, and looked away.

'That's good to hear. It's not nice when friends fall out. *Over nothing*!' She came to stand in front of us and made pop-eyes at me, still laughing. I really did blush then.

Me and Freddo and Aldo hadn't said anything about the day before. And now it looked like things had all blown over. I reckoned we felt it was best to forget about it. We were friends again. That's what mattered.

Plus the fact that the boys had managed to get out of the house without Mrs Moretti making them look for the missing puppet.

'Lucky!' Aldo had said. Now he was telling Lizzie. 'Robert's mam got a letter yesterday.'

'Who from, Rob? Your daddy?'

'No,' I said. 'From the Admiralty.'

'Saying what?' Lizzie looked a bit concerned. She didn't know if I was going to break some bad news.

'Nothing much,' I said. 'They still don't know where he is.'

'Oh, there's a worry,' said Lizzie. 'Fingers crossed he'll be back soon.'

'Yeah. Hope so,' I said, but I didn't know if I believed it.

'We haven't heard from Papa either,' said Aldo in a sad voice.

Freddo tried to brighten things up. 'Mamma thinks he'll be getting to Australia soon though, Al. He's been on that ship for a few weeks now.'

'Yes,' said Aldo. 'Then I can send him my letter.'

'Maybe,' said Freddo, looking at me. We both knew it was going to be difficult to get in touch with Mr Moretti.

'I'm going to tell him all about you, Lizzie,' said Aldo. 'And Captain. And the pigs.'

Lizzie laughed. 'I'm flattered, Al. I think. Now, how about a piece of Phil's beehive cake before we start work?'

'Yes please,' we nodded, and Lizzie went back into the house. We heard her talking to her father.

'Don't tell me,' he said, loud as anything to make sure we could hear. 'That bunch of layabouts from Tregwyn have turned up again for the free food.'

He came to the door and pretended he didn't know we were there. 'Oh sorry, boys. I didn't know you'd arrived. Bit early for you, innit?' He laughed at his own joke. So did we, because we were getting used to his jokes now.

Then Mr Morgan said, 'Right, I better get back to work. We got an inspector from the Ministry of Agriculture comin' tomorrow, so I got to go and make sure all the paperwork's in order.' He nodded at us. 'What are these three going to work on, Liz?'

It turned out the harvest was finished. 'Good and early,' said Mr Morgan as he went indoors. There was no more baling to be done. Cousin Phil and Idris were checking the stone walls down at the bottom of the valley. Bethan had the day off to visit her mam. There was no sign of the German prisoners.

So Lizzie decided, 'You can help me clean out the sty and the stables. Get some fresh hay in for Saturn.'

And that's what we did. Halfway through the morning, Freddo asked Lizzie, 'Where's the prisoners, then? In't they coming down?'

'Later on, supposed to, but they're keeping them up at the big house this morning. Don't know why.'

'Will Kristof be coming?' asked Aldo.

Freddo looked at me. I pretended to get on with my shovelling.

'Expect so, Al,' said Lizzie. 'He's got that puppet of yours, hasn't he?'

'Yes,' said Aldo. 'We got to get it back in the house today.'

'Oh, why's that?'

'Mamma wants to keep it in the kitchen till Papa comes home,' he told her, very serious. 'To remind us of him.'

'There's nice,' said Lizzie. 'I hope Kristof turns up, then.'

He didn't though. Not even when it got to dinner-time. That suited me. Things were definitely better between us three when he wasn't around.

Cousin Phil made the dinner. She had come back to the farm on the tractor with Idris. Captain sat on his lap when he drove it.

We sat round the big kitchen table and ate Phil's rabbit-and-leek pie. Captain lay under the table, spread flat across Aldo's feet. Now and again, Al would pass little bits of food to him when the others weren't looking. Only little bits, mind. Aldo wasn't keen on sharing too much of his dinner.

'What's happened to them Luftwaffe boys, then?' asked Idris. He was busy staring at his plate through his thick pebble glasses and mashing up his pie. He didn't have many teeth, I think, so he liked his food all squashy.

'I'm told they'll be down later,' said Mr Morgan. 'There's something going on up there though. Don't know what.'

Then he started to talk to Idris about the inspector who was coming the next day to check up on them. Cousin Phil and Lizzie joined in, so us boys were left to ourselves.

'What happens if they don't come, Fred?' Aldo was getting anxious. 'We got to get the puppet back today.'

'They will, Al. Don't worry,' said Freddo, but he was just saying that.

After dinner, we had to help Cousin Phil grind up the feed for the pigs. She made us work hard.

'Well, got to get as much out of you while we can,' she said, loud as ever. 'You'll be back at school before you know it.'

'Yes,' I said. 'Worse luck.'

'It's been great up here, aye,' said Freddo. 'Maybe, when school starts, we can come back in the afternoons, like.'

'Mamma will want us to help in the shop, Fred,' said Aldo. 'She's going to open up again,' he told Cousin Phil.

'Right you are,' she said. 'We'd better wait and see what happens, then, eh?'

126

After that, nobody said very much, except when Cousin Phil found out that I'd seen the bombers flying over the day before and wanted to know all about it. 'There's more and more of these daylight raids happening,' she said. 'According to the wireless, anyway. Expect there'll be more and more planes shot down too.'

'Hope so,' I said.

'Aye,' she agreed. 'They'll have to find somewhere else to put the pilots that bail out round here though. They won't be able to take many more up at the big house.'

The afternoon dragged on and still there was no sign of the prisoners.

Cousin Phil took us round the back of the farmhouse to finish off clearing the onion field, but Aldo was very fidgety. Every little noise and he'd leave off what he was doing and go and have a look in the yard.

'*Duw, Duw*, you got ants in your pants,' said Cousin Phil.

Freddo was getting anxious too, but he hid it better than his brother. He just went very quiet and concentrated on his work.

'They'll come, Fred,' I told him. 'Don' you worry.'

'I'm not,' he said, and went on pulling the onions up from the dry ground and throwing them in a basket.

Part of me hoped they wouldn't come. Then I wouldn't have to see Kristof again.

The other part did hope they'd come though, and that Kristof would bring the puppet, all mended. Then the boys could get it home and they wouldn't have to worry any more.

After a bit, Cousin Phil told us to lay off for the day. We'd done good work, she said. 'So you deserve a drink.'

She brought us three big glasses of the elderflower cordial that we'd had the first time we came to the farm. We sat on the bench by the door and drank it down. No one spoke.

'What's wrong with it, boys?' Cousin Phil shouted as she crossed the yard on her way to the pig shed.

'Nothing, Phil,' we said. 'It's lovely.'

It was too. Tasty as ever. But we all knew there'd be trouble in store for Freddo and Aldo when they got home.

We put our glasses down on the front step.

'Better be going, Al,' sighed Freddo. 'Kristof's not going to come now.'

'Let's just wait a bit more,' said Aldo. 'I bet he will.' He turned to me. 'He will, Rob, won't he?'

I didn't know what to say for the best. I paused. 'Well, it's getting a bit late, Al.'

'Come on,' said Fred, getting up from the bench and reaching out to give his brother a hand up. 'We've managed to keep Mamma from finding out what's happened up till now. We can do it one more night.'

Aldo held onto Freddo's hand and got to his feet. He wasn't happy, but there wasn't anything else we could do. The boys would have to go home and hope that Mrs Moretti didn't carry on about the puppet.

'Perhaps she'll have forgotten what she said, Al,' I told him, but, knowing Mrs Moretti, I didn't think that was very likely.

'We're going, Phil,' Freddo shouted.

She came to the door of the barn. 'Right you are.'

'See you tomorrow,' I said, getting up. 'Will you tell Mr Morgan and Lizzie?'

They were up in the top field, seeing to the baler. It was being picked up that day by another farmer.

'Right-o,' Cousin Phil shouted back. 'But you'll probably see them yourself when you go up the lane.'

'That's true,' I said. 'Ta-ta, then.'

The others joined in and Cousin Phil said, 'Thanks for your help, boys. With more like you, we'd win this war in a tick.' And off we went, out of the yard and towards the lane.

Nobody spoke.

When we passed by the wall outside the big house, the only signs of life were two of the soldiers spread out on the front steps. It looked like they were playing cards. Their rifles were resting by their sides.

'How be, boys? How y'doing?' they shouted. I was expecting them to joke about me courting Lizzie, but instead one of them said, 'Good grub today? What d'you get?'

'Rabbit pie,' said Aldo. 'With leeks. It was tasty. I had seconds.'

'I can see that,' one of them said, patting his stomach and pointing at him. They grinned and went on with their card game.

Freddo stopped in the lane and leaned over the wall. 'Why didn't you come down the farm earlier on?'

'Oh, can't tell you that,' said the soldiers, laughing. 'Top secret, that is.'

We knew it wasn't but they weren't going to tell us the real reason, so we carried on up the lane. We'd nearly left the big house behind when someone called out: 'Aldo! Freddo! Wait!'

The three of us turned and saw Kristof. He was standing at the top of the steps, waving his arms. 'Don't go,' he shouted. He waved harder now he knew we'd seen him.

The two soldiers had put down their cards. They sat up and reached for their rifles.

Aldo and Freddo began running back down the lane.

'Kristof!' Aldo shouted. 'We missed you.' He was waving too.

'What happened?' Freddo yelled. 'Where you been?'

Kristof didn't answer. Instead he was busy saying something to the soldiers. One of them stood up and said something back. Then he looked at his mate and they looked at Fred and Al. The man who had been speaking to Kristof gave him a nod and he went back inside the house. He called out to my friends as he went, 'Wait, please.'

I took a few steps down the lane. 'We ought to be going,' I said. 'We'll be late home.'

But Fred and Al weren't listening. They were standing right up against the wall, looking at the front door, waiting to see what would happen next.

Both soldiers were standing up, holding their rifles loosely across their chests.

'Aw, come on, Fred,' I shouted again, and edged a little bit nearer. 'Your mam'll be waiting for you.'

'Cool head, Rob,' Freddo shouted. 'Won't take a minute.' He didn't look at me when he said this. That made me a bit jealous again.

Kristof came out of the house. In his hand he was carrying the bag that belonged to Mr Moretti.

Aldo made a funny little noise, almost like a yelp. 'He's got the puppet, Fred.' He jumped up and down on the spot.

Kristof opened the bag and showed the soldiers what was inside. It looked like one of them told him to take the puppet out, because Kristof put the bag down on the top step and slowly lifted up the Pinocchio.

Even from where I was standing, I could see it was all in one piece. The arm and the leg were fixed, the nose stuck on.

Freddo and Aldo shouted for joy.

Kristof made the puppet bow and do a little jig to show how he was all mended.

My friends shouted even louder then and did a jig of their own.

'Thank you, Kristof,' Freddo shouted. 'Thank you.'

'You're great, you are,' Aldo yelled.

I just stood and watched.

The puppet finished dancing and Kristof folded it gently back into the bag. He put the bag over his shoulder and started to walk down the steps. One of the soldiers jumped in front of him and blocked the way with his rifle. 'Oi, Fritz!' I heard him shout. 'Where do you think you're going?'

Aldo called over the wall. 'His name's not Fritz. It's Kristof.'

It looked to me that Kristof thought he could just walk up to the wall and hand over the bag. But the soldiers weren't going to let him. He tried to take

131

another step down. The soldier pushed him back with his rifle.

Freddo and Al looked on, wide-eyed and quiet all of a sudden.

It was exciting, like watching a film. I didn't know what was going to happen. Maybe Kristof would get shot.

He spoke to the soldier at the bottom of the steps. Then he looked across to where my friends were waiting and nodded in their direction.

He took another step forward. The other soldier moved in behind him. Both of them raised their rifles a bit higher.

'Don't hurt him,' Aldo shouted. He was almost crying now. 'He's our friend.'

But the soldiers weren't listening. They were slowly moving Kristof back up the steps towards the front door. The one in front prodded him with his rifle to shift him along.

Kristof was still talking to them, and now Freddo called out, 'Please let him go. He's been kind to us. Honest, he has.'

Aldo said, 'He's mended our puppet.'

And Freddo added, 'Let him give it back to us. Please!'

The soldiers seemed to relax a little bit. They stopped pushing Kristof. Now one of them said something to his mate and then they both said something to Kristof.

He slipped the bag off his shoulder and handed it to the soldier who had blocked his way. He took it and nodded at his mate who raised his rifle a bit more to cover Kristof's back.

Aldo and Freddo were watching all this, still as statues, hardly breathing. I moved nearer, just a bit. I didn't want them to think I was that interested.

The soldier with the bag walked across the grass between the house and the wall where my friends were standing, waiting.

He lifted the bag over the wall. 'Now clear off!' I heard him say.

Freddo took the bag and handed it to Aldo. He cradled it to his chest, almost like it was a baby in a shawl.

'Go on,' the soldier said. 'Excitement over for today. Go home to your mams.'

'Thank you, Kristof,' Freddo called.

'Thank you,' Aldo echoed. 'See you soon.'

Kristof stood on the top of the steps and gave a little wave. The soldiers went to push him back inside but he shouted before he went. Just one word. 'Maybe.'

Freddo and Aldo came running up the lane to where I was standing. Excited they were, and happy. Aldo had slung the bag over his shoulder. It bounced up and down as he ran.

'Did you see that?' Freddo yelled. 'They wouldn't let Kristof give us the puppet.'

'That was mean, Rob, wasn't it?' Aldo came puffing up by his brother's side.

'He's a prisoner of war,' I said. 'They got to keep their eye on him.'

Freddo came to a stop, panting a bit, but still excited. 'Aw, come on, Rob. Give him credit. He mended the puppet, didn't he? Only natural he wanted to give it to us himself.'

133

'S'pose so,' I said, a bit grudging. I walked ahead up the lane. 'Can't just do what he likes though, can he?'

We didn't say much to each other after that, except every now and then Fred and Aldo would tell each other how great Kristof was for mending the puppet . . . and how kind he was . . . and how lucky he happened to be around at the right time.

The sun was almost ready to dip behind the side of the valley when we got to the top of the lane. Now Fred and Al couldn't wait to get home, fast, and smuggle the puppet into the house without their mam seeing.

We passed by the gate to the top field. Lizzie was there with her dad and Idris and another man. They were hitching up the baler to the man's tractor.

Lizzie looked up and saw us hurrying along the lane. 'Hey, you lot, aren't you going to say bye-bye?'

'Bye-bye,' Aldo shouted, then he stopped and lifted up the bag. 'We got our puppet back,' he said. 'Kristof mended it.'

'Told you he was good at fixing things, didn't we?' Lizzie came striding across the field, Captain in tow. When he saw Aldo he ran ahead and came snuffling round his feet, tail wagging.

Aldo patted him on the head and Captain gave him a big lick. That made Aldo giggle. 'It tickles,' he said.

'We can't stop, Lizzie,' said Freddo. 'Got to get home, see.'

'I'm not stopping you,' she laughed. 'Off you go.' She turned back into the field. 'See you tomorrow, will we?' She called over her shoulder. 'Looks like we'll be relying on you boys more and more.'

'Why's that?' I asked.

She stopped. 'Didn't Kristof tell you?'

'No,' said Freddo. 'They wouldn't let us speak to him.'

'No, of course,' she said. 'They're a bit jittery up the big house.'

Then she came back to where we were standing, all puzzled.

'The soldiers came to tell Daddy that he won't have the prisoners working for him any more. They'll be moving them out. New orders from the government, they said.'

'When they going?' Aldo asked, with a bit of a catch in his voice.

'Soon, I think,' said Lizzie. 'Next few days.'

'Where to?' asked Freddo.

'The Dominions,' said Lizzie. 'They're opening up camps in the Dominions.'

Chapter 21

'Kristof might be going to Australia!'

That was all Aldo could think about on our way home. 'Kristof might get to see Papa.'

'I keep telling you, Al, Australia's a big place,' said Freddo.

We were hurrying along, half running, half walking, because we were late and we all knew we'd cop it when we got home.

'I don't think there's much chance of them bumping into each other,' he said and gave me a wink. I liked that. It showed that we were still friends, even though I'd been a bit shirty when they were acting all grateful to Kristof.

'Anyway, Al,' I said. 'The Dominions isn't just Australia. It's Canada . . .'

'. . . and India,' said Freddo.

'. . . and . . . and . . .' I couldn't think of anywhere else, though Mr Rees, our teacher, had told us all about the countries in the Dominions.

'South Africa . . .' said Freddo. 'And . . . OOF!!' He bumped into Aldo who had stopped all of a sudden in the middle of the lane.

'I know that,' said Aldo. 'But I bet you anything they'll be sending the prisoners to Australia.'

'Right you are then,' said Freddo. He nudged his brother along and gave me another wink. 'If you say so.'

Once Aldo got something into his head, it was difficult

to shift him. Now and then, he would mutter something about Kristof meeting his dad, but it was more to himself than to us.

The sun was much lower in the sky by the time we got back to our village. The shops had all closed up, but there were still some people around.

There was a George Formby film on at the cinema. Gwenda Lewis was going in with her mother. We crossed over to the other side of the street, hoping she wouldn't notice us.

She did. 'Hello,' she shouted. 'Haven't seen much of you boys lately.'

'No,' we said. 'We been busy.'

'Over that Tŷ Cornant place, I suppose,' said Gwenda. Her mother pulled her up the steps to the cinema, telling her to shush. 'Come on, dear,' she said, 'or we'll miss the start of the big picture.' Then they were through the glass door and out of view.

Freddo stopped. 'How the hell did she know about Tŷ Cornant?'

'I dunno,' I said, walking on, feeling guilty. I knew that Vic and Billy must have told her. And if Gwenda knew about our special place, there was a good chance that Ivor and his butties did too.

Freddo caught up with me. 'That girl knows everything,' he said. 'She'd make a good spy.'

'No,' I said. 'She's too chopsy. She'd never be able to keep a secret.'

Freddo laughed. 'True enough.' He tugged Aldo along because he was flagging a bit. 'Come on, Al,' he said. 'Nearly home.'

'Yes,' puffed Aldo. 'How we goin' to get the puppet in, Fred? Without Mamma seeing.'

'Don't worry, Al,' said Freddo. 'I've thought of a way.'

I don't think he had, though, because he gave me a sort of HELP! look that Aldo couldn't see.

By the time we got to their shop, mind, he'd come up with an idea. 'You go round the yard door, Al,' he said, 'and wait for me to come and open it. Rob will keep Mamma busy in the shop.'

'Will I?' I said. 'How?'

'Oh . . . tell her something else about the letter you got about your dad.'

'There's nothing else to tell.'

'Well make it up, mun.'

He sent Aldo down the road at the side of their shop, and when he was safely out of sight, Freddo knocked on the closed front door.

'Who is it?' Mrs Moretti called out, checking first before she would come to open it.

'It's us, Mamma,' Freddo called. 'Sorry we're late.'

'You are,' I could hear her say as she came though the café. 'This isn't fair, you know.' She unbolted the door. 'I worry when you're out so long.' She put her hand to her chest all of a sudden. 'Where's your brother?'

'He's fine, Mamma. But his daps are all covered in muck from the pig shed. He's gone to swill it off in the back yard.' He squeezed in past her. 'I'll just get the key and let him in.'

Mrs Moretti narrowed her eyes and watched him go. 'Why didn't he just take them off and come through the shop?'

'You know how stubborn he is,' said Freddo. 'When he makes up his mind . . .'

He was through the café before she could say anything else, but he shouted back: 'Rob's got something to tell you.'

'What's that, Robert?' she said, turning back to face me.

'Ummm . . .' I said.

She looked at me, waiting.

'Mmmm . . .' I said again.

'Well . . .? Is it about your papa?'

'Er . . . yes . . .'

'Have you had more news?'

'Not really, no.' I didn't want to lie to her.

'So . . . what do you want to tell me?'

In the distance, I could hear the sound of a door slamming. Did that mean Aldo was safely in the house?

'I . . . er . . .'

'Maybe you could tell me another time, eh?' she said, losing patience a bit. 'I better go and see if Aldo's cleaned his daps.'

She made to close the door. I panicked. Had I given the boys enough time to get the puppet back in the house? 'Mrs Moretti . . .' I said, a bit desperate.

'Yes, Robert. Be quick now, there's a good boy. If there's nothing you want to tell me, maybe there's something you want to ask, eh?'

Of course! 'Yes,' I said. 'There is.'

'Go on then.'

'Well . . . um . . . they would have told us if my dad was . . . if there was anything . . . wrong. Wouldn't they?'

'The Admiralty people, you mean?'

139

'Yes.'

'I'm sure they would have,' she said. 'So you mustn't give up hope. We haven't.'

'Right,' I said. 'I won't.'

From the kitchen there came the sound of footsteps pounding.

Mrs Moretti called out. 'What are you up to, boys?'

Freddo shouted back. 'Nothing!'

'Mm!' said Mrs Moretti. 'A very noisy nothing.' She closed the door a bit more. 'It's blackout soon. You better be going.' She smiled. 'Good night, Roberto.' That was what Mr Moretti used to call me.

'Yes,' I said. 'Thank you, Mrs Moretti.'

I stepped back, ready to take off down the street. Mission accomplished, I hoped.

More heavy footsteps on the stairs, then Aldo came bustling out of the kitchen and through the shop.

'Mamma,' he laughed. 'You won't believe what I found under all the shoes in my cupboard.' He gave a great big grin and from behind his back – just like a magician – he brought out his father's puppet.

Chapter 22

I thought I would get a real telling-off when I got home.

I knew how late I was when I saw that Mam had already put our blackout curtains up.

But she didn't say anything. Nor Nanna, neither.

That's because they were busy at the table in the kitchen. The yellowy gas lamp hissed away above them. Mam was sitting, writing. With a pen in her hand, her head was bent low over the pad. She was concentrating hard.

Nanna was next to her, chewing on something, and nodding. 'That's good, Myra,' she was saying when I came through the kitchen door. 'He'd like to hear about that.'

'I'm back,' I said, moving over to the table and sliding into a chair across from my mam. 'Who you writing to?'

'Your father,' she said, looking up. 'Who else?'

For a moment I thought they must have heard from him. Then I realised that they'd be looking a lot happier if they had.

'Sorry I was so upset last night,' my mam said. 'I was a bit nervy with it all.' She smiled.

I smiled back.

Nanna nodded.

'I'm in much better shape today,' said Mam. 'So, even though we don't know where your dad is, I thought I'd write him another letter anyway. Let's just hope the Admiralty people can get it to him this time.'

I thought she was putting on a brave face. This must have been the sixth or seventh letter she'd sent since Dad went off to Norway, and we'd heard nothing back. Where did all the letters go? I wondered.

'You write something, Robert.' Mam pushed the pad across the table.

'I don't know what to say.'

Nanna grunted. 'Tell him about the farm.' She gave a little sniff. 'You spend more time there than you do here.' She fumbled for something in her apron pocket and brought out a hanky to dab her mouth.

'All right,' I said.

Mam handed me the pen. 'And tell him how much you miss him.'

'Yes,' I said. I looked down at the paper quickly because I could feel my eyes begin to sting. 'Aldo's written a letter to his dad,' I added, wondering how to start.

'Have he got to Australia then?' Nanna asked.

'Not yet, no. But Aldo's got a letter ready for when they know where he is.'

'Aw, bless him. He's a kind-hearted boy.'

'He is,' Mam agreed. 'It'll be difficult to get it to Pietro though. I don't think the Red Cross will help.'

'No, they won't,' I said. 'But Mrs Moretti says they'll find a way, so that's enough for Aldo. Bit daft, if you ask me.'

I started to write.

'Now, now, Robert,' Mam said. 'If it makes the boy feel better, then there's no harm, is there?'

'You're right, My,' said Nanna. 'Maybe it do help him feel a bit closer to his father.' She tucked her hanky in her apron pocket. 'Got to find ways to keep all these missing people in our thoughts, see, boy.'

'Yes, Nanna,' I said, but I didn't feel that writing this letter to Dad brought him any closer. He felt as far away as ever.

'Right,' said Mam. She got up from the table. 'How about a cuppa?'

'Lovely,' said Nanna. 'I'm parched with all this writing.'

Mam looked at me and raised her eyebrows. She was smiling. It was good to see. 'Get on with it, Robert,' she said. 'Or the war will be over by the time you finish.'

'I wish it was,' I said, but I put the pen to paper and started to tell Dad all about Tŷ Cornant.

I told him about riding on the tractor, and helping to bring in the hay. I told him about the new piglets and Cousin Phil's cooking. I didn't tell him about Kristof though. And, anyway, I'd never told Mam and Nanna about the prisoners of war either, in case the two of them stopped me from going up there.

I tried to follow the lines on the pad, but I wasn't the best at handwriting. The words sloped off the page. It took me a while to finish what I wanted to say.

'Missing you, Dad,' I wrote at the end. 'Come home soon. Your loving son, Robert.'

I put an X to sign off.

Then it was time for bed.

I went to sleep very quick that night and I only woke once in the dark.

Somewhere, quite far away, there was the sound of bombing and the rattle of the ack-ack guns. I peeked out from behind the blackout curtain and stared into the darkness. Above the ridge of the valley, there was a patch of light in the sky, red and flickering, over Swansea way. Exciting it was, and scary. The searchlights criss-crossed each other, searching out the bombers.

Out there, people were getting killed or injured in the raid. I couldn't understand why Freddo and Aldo could forget that. How could they get so friendly with one of the men who might have been doing the bombing if he hadn't been taken prisoner?

All right, I know he was just obeying orders. Like my dad, as Aldo had said. It was all very confusing and I had trouble getting back to sleep for a while. I made a promise though, before I dropped off.

If I wanted to stay best friends with Freddo and Aldo, I knew I was going to have to stop getting jealous when they got pally with Kristof.

Looked like he'd be gone soon, anyway.

Good riddance!

Chapter 23

Just after nine o'clock next morning my butties called for me.

Mam had already gone to work.

'Who's that now?' Nanna asked when they knocked on our front door. She was settled in her chair, cwtched up to the wireless as usual.

'It'll be Fred and Al, Nanna,' I said. 'They've come for me to go up Tŷ Cornant.'

I scooted along the passage and out of the house before she had time to go on about spending too much time at the farm. 'See you later, Nanna.'

As soon as I slammed the front door shut, Freddo grabbed hold of my arm, very excited. 'We got something to tell you, Rob,' he said. He had a big grin on his face.

Not Aldo though. He looked like he'd been crying. I thought that maybe their mam had found out about the puppet getting broken, but it wasn't that.

'Papa's ship has arrived in Australia,' said Freddo. He was fit to burst with the news.

'Aw, that's great, Fred.' I put my arm round his shoulder to give him a sort of squeeze. 'How d'you know?'

'Aunty Edda got a phone call from her cousins in Glasgow. Someone told them.'

Aldo burst into tears.

'Why you crying, Al?' I asked. 'It's good, innit?'

He sniffed and wiped his nose on his shirt sleeve. 'Tell

Rob what Aunty Edda said. About what it was like on the ship.'

'Rob don't want to hear that, Al,' said Freddo and walked away towards the short cut up the *gwli* at the end of our street. 'I told you to forget it, didn't I?'

'Forget what?' I asked.

Freddo stopped. 'Aunty Edda's cousins told her how bad things had been on the *Dunera*.'

'It was terrible, Rob,' said Aldo, a bit choked. 'Too crowded, see.'

'Leave it be now, Al,' said Freddo. 'The good news is that they've got there.'

But Aldo had the story fixed in his mind and wouldn't leave it alone. 'They kept the men below deck nearly all the time,' he said. 'They screwed up the portholes so they didn't have no fresh air or light.'

Then Freddo couldn't help himself. He had to join in. 'They had to sleep on the floor on straw mattresses.'

And now the story tumbled out and they took it in turns to tell me. 'There weren't enough lavs,' said Aldo.

'The food was really bad,' said Freddo.

'There were maggots in the bread.'

'They had to drink seawater.'

'The guards beat people up . . . and took their money and their belongings.'

'. . . and their letters.' Aldo stopped and fumbled around in the back pocket of his shorts.

'What you after?' asked Freddo.

'This!' said Aldo and, pleased as Punch, he took out the envelope addressed to his father. It was very crumpled, but he waved it in the air and said, 'Now I've definitely got to find a way to get this to Papa. He needs some good news.' He didn't look upset any more. He looked pleased. And determined.

'Definitely,' he said again. He folded up the letter very carefully and put it in his pocket.

Freddo nodded, but didn't say anything and we marched on up the *gwli*.

'I bet your mam's happy,' I said. 'Did she say anything about the puppet?'

'Only that she was glad I found it,' said Aldo. 'She's put it on the sideboard in the kitchen. To remind us of Papa.'

'Didn't she suspect anything?'

Freddo thought she had. 'She didn't half give me a funny look, aye. But she was pleased all the same.'

'It was a happy ending,' said Aldo. 'Thanks to Kristof.'

'Yeah. He mended it really well,' said Freddo.

We were nearly at the top of the *gwli* now, just where it opened out on the hillside. I changed the subject.

'Did you hear the raid last night?'

'No,' said Aldo. 'Where was it, Rob?'

'Over Swansea way, I think. It was big though. You could see the light from the flames.'

'Must have been lots of planes,' said Freddo. 'D'you see any get shot down?'

'Too far away,' I said. 'But our guns were firing like mad, so I bet they did. Hope so!'

I meant it too.

The village fell away below us as we charged on over the tumpy grass.

'There's Billy and Vic,' said Aldo, stopping to take a bit of a breather.

'Wonder if they know about Tŷ Cornant?' said Freddo, stopping too. 'Bet Gwenda's told them already.'

'Most likely,' I said, not wanting to talk about it. 'I wonder what we'll be doing today? Up the farm.'

We stood and watched Billy and Vic. They were kicking a tin around on the bottom field. That's where the pit ponies used to have their two weeks of fresh air when the colliery closed for the summer holidays.

'Well, first I'm going to give this to Kristof,' said Aldo. He pulled out his precious letter again. 'That's what I'm gonna do.' He looked very pleased with himself. 'I'm going to ask him to give this to Papa when he meets him in Australia.'

I burst out laughing. I couldn't help it.

'What's so funny, Rob?' Aldo asked. He tried to smooth out the envelope a bit by rubbing it flat on his leg.

Freddo gave me a look. I could tell he was angry with me for laughing at his brother. I stopped.

'Aw . . . well . . . it's just that we keep telling you Australia's a big place, Al. And you don't know where your dad's going to end up yet.'

Aldo's head dropped so he didn't have to look at me. He folded the envelope and put it back in his pocket.

'Anyway, you don't know if Kristof *is* going to be sent to Australia,' I said. 'It's a bit loopy, mun. Be honest.'

'*He* believes it,' said Freddo, very quiet, staring me straight in the eye. 'It's his little dream. So there's no harm in it, is there?'

'S'pose not,' I said, a bit sulky. I walked on up the hill.

Freddo came striding along after me. We left Aldo behind, looking a bit confused and upset. I was sorry about that. I didn't want to hurt him. But I thought it was a stupid idea and so did Freddo, really. He was daft to let Aldo think it would work.

'Where does he think Kristof and your dad will meet?' I whispered to Freddo when he caught me up. 'In a café somewhere? It's *twp*, innit?'

We faced each other, both of us a bit angry.

'Not in a café, no. You're being *twp* now,' said Freddo. He was whispering too, so Aldo wouldn't hear. 'But if Kristof is sent to Australia, he's going to end up in a camp, in' he? So is Papa. Who knows . . . it might be the same one.'

He calmed down a bit. 'That's what Aldo thinks, anyway.' He looked down the hill to where Aldo was standing watching Billy and Vic. 'So, I'm gonna go along with it. To keep him happy. Can't you?'

I wanted to say, 'No, I think it's a mad idea.' But it wouldn't be true, not altogether. I did think it was mad. But I knew my real reason. It was because it involved Kristof.

Aldo had walked up to where we were standing. He had obviously heard what we were saying because he said to me, 'Kristof will do his best to get the letter to Papa. I know he will.'

'You and your blinkin' Kristof,' I said. 'I'm fed up with hearing about him . . . how clever he is . . . and all that. You think he's great, don' you, Al? But you're daft to trust him . . . He's our enemy. Why should he help you?'

Aldo looked at me, hurt. Tears filled his eyes. 'Because he's kind, Rob. You know that.'

'I give up, honest I do,' I said. 'I think it's stupid, so there.'

Freddo punched me on the arm. Hard.

It didn't hurt, though. It just took me by surprise.

I think it took Freddo by surprise too. 'Don't say no more, Rob,' he growled. Then he came even closer and said, 'He's upset enough as it is. Don't be mean. Not today.'

'I'm not being mean. I'm just being truthful. And you know it.' I started to walk on up the hill.

Then I stopped suddenly. 'I'm going home,' I said and turned round to head back to the village. I don't know why, but I did.

'Who's being stupid now then?' Freddo shouted.

Aldo looked confused. 'Don't go, Rob. What'll we tell Lizzie?'

'Tell her anything. I don't care.' I was almost running now. Things had got out of control and I didn't know why. I just wanted to be gone.

I ran on down the hill. 'Billy!' I shouted. 'Vic! What you playing?'

Chapter 24

'Just having a kick about,' Billy said, chipping the tin into the bushes as I got to them.

'Why in't you with Freddo and Al?' Vic asked.

'Getting fed up with doing the same thing every day,' I lied. 'Felt like doing something different. They didn't.'

'Oh, aye,' Billy said. 'So they've gone up that Tŷ Cornant, have they?'

'S'pose so,' I said. I wanted to change the subject. The farm was still our special place and I didn't want anyone else poking their noses in.

'No point in asking if you want to come over the Pandy, is there?' Billy asked.

'No,' I said.

'Right,' said Billy. He kicked a clump of dry grass my way. I passed it back. He lobbed it on to Vic. Then he said, all of a sudden, 'Let's go and play in Gwenda Lewis's air-raid shelter.'

'How can we do that?' I asked. 'She won't let us.'

'She will,' said Vic.

'She said we could go and play up there any time we liked,' Billy said. He laughed. 'I think she got a crush on Vic.'

'Come off it,' Vic said, sheepish. 'She haven't.'

'Reckon she has, Vic,' Billy went on. 'Must have liked it when you tickled her leg, see.'

We all laughed at that, remembering how we'd tried to

scare Gwenda in the darkness of the shelter. That was the day that Mr Moretti's puppet had got broken.

'What do you reckon?' said Billy. 'Be a bit of fun, won' it?'

'All right,' I said. 'Just for a while, mind.'

I wasn't very keen to be going up Gwenda's house, but I didn't want to be left by myself. Didn't want to spend my time thinking about the way I'd behaved to Freddo and Al. It was a bit babyish, really. Just like Lizzie said.

So, we set off for Gwenda's, eyes peeled in case Ivor and his friends were around, ready to get in on the act.

'Will you tell me something?' I said, when we got to the bottom of the steps leading up to Gwenda's front door.

'What?' said Billy, taking the steps two at a time.

'Did you ever say anything to Gwenda about Tŷ Cornant?'

Billy went leaping ahead. No answer.

'Did you, though?' I called after him.

'What if I did?' Billy stopped and turned to look down at me.

'Nothing. Just wanted to know if you told her. That's all.'

By my side, Vic pretended he had something in his eye. He tried to wipe it away.

'Might have,' Billy said, a bit shifty. 'By accident, like. Did she tell you I did?'

'No. But I thought it must have been you, 'cos we never told anyone else about it.'

'Why's it so special anyway?' Billy asked, jumping back down the steps.

'Dunno, really,' I said. 'It's only a farm, but we had a good time up there and we didn't want anyone else to come along and spoil it.'

'We wouldn't spoil it,' Vic said.

'No. But other people might,' I said.

'Like Ivor and his butties, you mean?'

'Yes. Do you think he knows?'

'Dunno,' said Billy and went on up the steps.

'Dunno,' echoed Vic, pushing past, following.

It looked to me like they might have told Ivor, but I didn't want to pick any more arguments that day, so I left it at that. I did the steps two at a time and caught up with them by the front door.

'Who's going to knock, then?' I asked, puffing a bit.

'Gwenda said to go straight round the back,' said Billy and he led the way down the side of the house along the little alley that led to the garden.

'Gwen,' he called, as he went. 'Are you in?'

No one answered.

We stood at the edge of the big garden. Mr Lewis had dug up more of the grass to plant new vegetables.

'*Duw*,' said Billy. 'There'll be enough here to feed the whole of Wales soon.'

There was still no sign of life, so Vic called out this time: 'Gwenda. You there?'

No reply.

'Her mam and dad can't be in,' I said. 'Or they'd have shooed us away by now.'

'Perhaps she's in the shelter,' said Billy. 'She might not be able to hear us. Come on.' And he set off down the garden, winding his way through the vegetable beds.

'You'll cop it,' Vic hissed, in a loud whisper.

'No, I won't,' Billy said, half turning. 'We been invited, haven't we?'

'Fair enough,' Vic said, and the two of us followed on.

All the time, I was expecting a voice behind us to shout out and ask what we were doing, but no one did.

Billy knocked on the metal roof of the shelter. 'Anybody home?' he called.

No answer.

'Let's have a look inside,' said Billy, and before we could stop him he'd jumped down the steps to where the thick curtain was covering the front door.

'Gwenda!' he called again. He lifted up the curtain. 'You got visitors,' he said, and poked his head inside. 'Get the kettle on.'

He popped his head out again. 'No one here. Let's go in and wait for her. Give her a bit of a fright.'

Me and Vic weren't too sure.

'Aw, come on,' said Billy. 'Just for a laugh.'

I looked at Vic. We nodded at each other. 'Right-o!' we said and jumped down the steps.

Inside, the shelter was as smelly as it was before. It was dark too, until your eyes got used to it. 'Put the light on, Bill,' I said as we sat on the little benches along the walls, me and Vic on one side, Billy on the other.

'It's gone,' said Billy, reaching up for where the light switch used to be. 'The electric fire have too.' He laughed. 'See, my Uncle Tecwyn was right. I told Gwenda it was against the rules to have electricity in these shelters. Someone must have told Gwenda's father to take it out.'

154

Me and Vic smiled, enjoying the thought of someone telling Mr Lewis off for once.

Then we sat and waited. I tried to imagine what my friends were doing. They probably weren't even up at the farm yet, what with the way Aldo dawdled along. It always took us the best part of an hour to get to Tŷ Cornant. So they wouldn't have managed to see Kristof, and Aldo wouldn't have told him his stupid idea and asked him to be postman.

I stood up. 'I better be going. My nanna'll be needing her dinner.'

That was just an excuse. I didn't want to play any more.

'We'll come with you,' Billy said. 'I'm hungry too.'

'Me too,' said Vic and the three of us jostled our way out of the shelter and up the steps.

Then we heard voices, girls' voices, coming from by the house.

'It's Gwenda,' hissed Billy. 'Quick! Back in the shelter. Jump out on her!'

Too late. It *was* Gwenda and she'd seen us. She had Margaret Williams with her from two classes down. I expect she could boss her around more easily.

'I've been looking for you, Robert Prosser,' Gwenda shouted, marching through the garden to where we were standing. 'I didn't expect to find you here though.'

The cord of her gas-mask box had tightened round her neck a bit as she'd marched along. She worked it loose and straightened out the box by her side. 'I heard you weren't going up Tŷ Cornant.'

See, she knew everything, did Gwenda.

'What's it to you?' I asked.

'I had something important to tell you,' Gwenda said. 'But if that's your attitude, I won't.' She linked arms with Margaret. 'Come on, Maggie,' she said, all swanky, pushing past us. 'Let's leave them guessing.'

She dragged Margaret down the steps to the shelter door.

'Aw, play fair, Gwen,' said Billy. 'You can't leave it like that.'

'I can,' said Gwenda, lifting up the curtain and pushing Margaret inside the shelter. 'If he doesn't want to know about his mates, then I can't be bothered to tell him.'

She poked her head through the curtain and went on talking to her new friend, very exaggerated, about making herself comfy on the benches. We all knew that she was bursting to tell us what she'd found out.

'Go on, Gwen,' I said. 'Tell us. I didn't mean to be rude.'

She stopped talking to Margaret and drew her head back out of the shelter. 'They're going be in dead trouble,' she said, 'the Moretti boys.'

My heart bumped a bit. 'Why? What's happened?'

'Nothing yet. But it will.'

She was enjoying this.

'What do you mean?'

'They've found out where you and Freddo and Aldo slip off to these days.'

'Who's "they"?' I asked. But I knew.

'Ivor Ingrams and his friends,' she said, very chirpy now she'd delivered her news. 'They're going to follow them.'

I looked at Billy. He pretended to be very interested in the vegetable beds. Vic too.

They *had* told Ivor.

'And . . . ?' I said.

'Well, when they see which way they go, they're going to lie in wait for them on the way back. Ivor says he's got a fight to finish.' She turned away, lifting the curtain higher to go inside the shelter.

'Thought you might like to know,' she said. 'Lucky you decided not to go with them, wasn't it?'

'I'm going now,' I said, already on the move through the garden. 'Bill? Vic? You coming?'

I stopped.

They looked at each other.

'You owe me this,' I said.

Billy nodded at Vic. 'Why not?'

And, quick as a flash, we shot along to the side of the house.

Then I thought of something. I stopped and turned round. Gwenda was watching us from the doorway. 'Thanks, Gwen,' I shouted. 'Thanks for the warning.'

'Oh,' she shouted back, all surprised. 'Just doing my bit, that's all. You don't deserve it though.' She popped inside the shelter.

Then, quick as anything, she popped her head out again and yelled: 'I'd get a move on if I were you. Ivor and his friends set off ages ago.'

Chapter 25

It looked like we were too late.

By the time we caught up with Freddo and Aldo on the lane to Tŷ Cornant, they weren't by themselves. Tagging along behind was a group of about eight kids, with Ivor in the lead.

I couldn't see who was with him but I reckoned there were a few boys from our class. The rest were evacuees.

Most likely, Freddo and Aldo had found out they were being followed, so Ivor and his butties had decided to come out in the open.

We'd come running round a bend in the lane when we saw them up ahead.

We skidded to a halt. They hadn't noticed us yet, so we dropped to the ground behind a gorse bush. We were panting fit to bust, we'd run so fast.

'Let's see what happens,' Billy said, trying to get his breath.

Nothing much, it looked like.

Freddo and Aldo kept walking along. Ivor's gang followed. They were yelling and laughing, but we couldn't hear what they were saying. Now and then one of the kids would run ahead of my friends and shout something to their faces.

'What we going to do?' Vic whispered, breathing hard. 'Dunno.'

Billy had an idea. 'If we get behind the wall we could creep up on them.'

'Good thinking,' said Vic.

'Right,' I said. 'Make sure no one's looking this way though.'

We hung on a bit to get our breath back, then, careful not to be seen, we nipped over the wall one by one. Keeping low, and moving slow and quiet through the rough grass, we got near enough to hear what was happening.

Ivor's lot were teasing my friends about their mother.

'Got to report to the police, ain't she?' one of the evacuees said.

'That's 'cos she's a spy,' another one said.

'No, she's not!' I heard Freddo reply, not loud, but angry. 'Don't talk rot.'

'Bet she is,' said someone else.

'Yeah. And so's that Aunty Ella . . .' another voice piped up.

'Edda!' said the first boy. 'Edda!'

They began to chant her name. 'Ed-da! Ed-da! Ed-da!'

'Stop it,' Freddo shouted. He was really angry now.

All the time, the little group was moving further up the lane. We hung back behind the wall but moved along with them.

'Are you spies too?' That was Ivor. 'Is that why you've kept this Tŷ Cornant place so hush-hush? You and your little butty Robert.'

They all laughed at that.

I could tell Billy and Vic were staring at me, wondering how I'd react. I felt my face burn red, but I didn't do anything.

'Where is he then, Titch Prosser?' Ivor went on, jeering like. 'Off on a spying mission of his own, is he?'

'Don't be stupid,' said Freddo. 'We're not spies. None of us.'

And Aldo piped up for the first time. 'We're just going to help our friends on the farm.'

'Aw, there's nice.' Ivor was all sarcastic now. 'What's their names then?'

'Lizzie,' said Aldo.

There were some wolf whistles at that.

'And Phil,' Aldo went on. 'And Mr Morgan . . .'

'That's enough, Al,' said Freddo.

'And Kristof . . .'

From where we were, crouched down behind the wall, Billy and Vic looked at me, eyes wide.

'*Who's he?*' Billy mouthed.

I shook my head and mouthed back, '*Tell you later.*'

We could hear that the group had stopped moving. Some of the boys must have run on in front of Freddo and Aldo to block their way.

'Kris-tof!' Ivor was saying now. 'What kind of name is that?'

'Sounds German to me,' someone said.

'Yeah,' they agreed. 'It's a Jerry name, innit?'

'Is *he* a spy then?' I recognised Trevor Davies's voice. Trust him to tag along with Ivor.

'Is that where you go to meet him?' Ivor again. 'To pass messages, like?'

'No,' said Freddo.

'You're traitors, you are,' one of the evacuees said.

'No we're not,' Freddo snarled. 'Get out of our way.'

'I don't think so,' Ivor said. 'We don't let traitors pass, do we, boys?'

'No,' they shouted and by the sound of it I could tell that they were beginning to jostle Freddo and Aldo.

Aldo whimpered, 'Let us go. We haven't done nothin' wrong.'

'He's crying again,' someone said.

'*That's Evan Griffiths,*' I whispered to Billy. He was in our class too.

'Aldo needs his dolly,' said someone else.

There was a lot of laughing at that, and then Trevor Davies started up another chant: 'Traitors! Traitors! Traitors!'

They all joined in, laughing and jeering.

'Come on, Al,' I heard Freddo say.

There was the sound of scuffling. Most likely, they were trying to push through the crowd. Footsteps pounded away up the lane. Then there was a big shout: 'Get him, Ive!'

I looked at Billy and Vic. '*I'm going to see what's happening.*'

'*Careful,*' Vic said.

Of course I was careful.

I stood up very slowly until my head was level with the big, loose stones on the top of the wall. I shifted two of them aside so I could get a view of what was going on. None of Ivor's gang noticed. They were all too busy.

A little way up the lane, some of the boys had Aldo pinned against the wall. Aldo was strong, so it took six of them to hold him. One of the kids had climbed up on the wall and was hanging onto his hair. Aldo was struggling

161

as hard as he could and growling and trying to kick out, but he couldn't break free.

Further on, Ivor and one of the evacuees had grabbed hold of Freddo's arms. They were trying to get him against the wall too. He was wriggling and squirming, but Ivor was much bigger, so he couldn't break free either.

One of the kids holding onto Aldo held up his hand and waved what looked like a piece of paper.

'Look what I found,' he shouted.

It was Aldo's letter to his father.

'It's a secret message,' the boy said.

The others jumped up and down in excitement. 'What's in it? What's it say?'

Aldo struggled even harder to break free. The boy holding onto his hair yanked his head back against the wall.

Colin Vickers from our class grabbed hold of the envelope. 'It's got another foreign name on it,' he shouted.

'It's my father's, *twpsyn*!' Freddo shouted, but they ignored him.

'Blimey,' yelled one of the evacuees. 'They got a regular little spy network going, these two.'

There was lots of laughter.

'Give it back,' Aldo moaned. 'It's private. For my papa.'

'*He's* a traitor as well,' said Colin. 'That's why the police took him away.'

'That's a lie!' Freddo shouted. 'Our father's not a traitor. Give the letter back.'

That made them even more excited.

Trevor grabbed hold of the envelope. 'Let's open it!' he said. 'Let's see what he's written.'

'No!' Aldo cried. 'Don't open it. It's private.'

One of the kids let go of Aldo for a minute. It looked like he was going to rip open the envelope. 'Shall I, Ive?' he called.

'Why not?' Ivor called back, puffing a bit with the effort of holding onto Freddo. 'Even if there's no secret message, it'll give us a laugh.'

'No!' Freddo yelled, and yanked himself out of Ivor's grip.

The other boy let go too and Freddo legged it up the lane towards Aldo. 'I'm coming, Al,' he shouted.

'ME TOO!!'

I was amazed at how loud my voice sounded as I jumped up on the wall.

Everybody turned to look and, in the surprise, Freddo pulled at the boys surrounding Aldo and tried to tear them away.

I leapt down off the wall and started running to help him. Behind me, I could hear Billy and Vic following.

'Look out, boys,' Ivor yelled. He stood in the middle of the lane, a smirk on his face. 'The cavalry's arrived. We're done for now.'

His gang jeered and laughed, but I didn't care. Freddo neither. We pitched into the group round Aldo and tried to pull him free. Billy and Vic were there too, pulling and scuffling.

I got smacked in the face. By Colin Vickers, I think. I wanted to cry because it hurt, but I wasn't going to let them see that.

Someone tugged at my arm and sent me spinning across the lane.

I ran back but Ivor stood in my way and gave me

another push. We were coming out of this badly. Aldo was still pinned against the wall. So was Freddo now. Me and Vic and Billy were like terriers yapping around, but none of us was having much effect.

Suddenly we heard a voice call out from further up the lane: 'Hey!'

It was Lizzie, striding along in her blue dungarees.

Then an even louder voice, booming out like a foghorn. 'WHAT THE HECK IS GOING ON HERE?'

Everybody froze for a moment. Like they were turned to stone. By Cousin Phil. Her big, loud voice had taken them all by surprise.

And before they could start up again, Lizzie shouted, 'See them off, Captain!'

The dog came bounding along the lane, tail wagging, teeth bared, ready to round up Ivor's lot.

Some of the boys let go of Aldo and Fred and backed away, a bit nervous. Aldo struggled free of the rest. He gave his head such a big shake that the boy holding his hair lost his grip – and his balance. He tipped backwards over the wall. 'Oww!' he said, as he landed. Must have fallen in the gorse prickles.

Best of all, Ivor began to march off down the lane towards our village.

'Ive,' Trevor called, looking a bit left behind. 'Where you goin'?'

'Don't trust that dog,' said Ivor. He turned and ran backwards so he could keep an eye on Captain. 'It's got a bad look.'

Captain was in the middle of the scrum now, growling but not biting.

'That'll do, boy,' said Lizzie. 'That'll do.'

Ivor's lot started to run down the lane after him. The kid who had fallen off the wall jumped back over to join them. His legs were all scratched.

'We'll pay you back, don't worry,' Trevor shouted as he went. Some of the others joined in.

'Well, you'll have me to deal with,' Cousin Phil yelled at them. 'Go home, you horrible little boys.'

A couple of them stuck their tongues out. Straight off, she stuck hers out too.

Captain gave a few barks to send them on their way.

'There, Captain,' said Lizzie. 'Good dog.'

He gave a growl and came over to lick Aldo's hand.

'Well, that was exciting,' said Lizzie, watching Ivor and his friends swaggering down the lane, making it look as if nothing had happened. 'Handy we came to look for you. We wondered if you were going to turn up today.' Then she nodded at Billy and Vic. 'These your friends?' she asked.

'Yes,' I said. 'They are. For definite.'

Billy and Vic looked pleased.

'That's nice,' said Lizzie. 'It's good to have friends.' She looked at me when she said it. 'People who'll stick by you, no matter what.'

She bent down to pick something up. An envelope.

Freddo whispered to me, 'Thanks. I didn't expect to see you.'

'Well, I'm here,' I muttered. I didn't want to say any more, but I was pleased I was there. With my friends. I felt good. A bit bruised though.

'Is this yours, Freddo?' Lizzie waved the envelope in

the air. It was very crumpled and very grubby. 'I found it on the ground. It's got your family name on it.'

'It's mine,' said Aldo, pleased as anything.

Lizzie handed it over. 'You'd better all come down the farm and get cleaned up,' she said. 'Then you can tell us what that was all about.'

'They wanted to read my letter,' said Aldo, rubbing his head where he'd had his hair pulled.

'Who's it to?' Cousin Phil asked.

'Papa,' he said. 'We better get it to Kristof now.'

Lizzie and Cousin Phil gave him a curious look.

'I'll explain,' said Freddo. 'On the way down.' He looked at me as if he expected me to say what I thought about Aldo's idea. Well, I still thought it was daft, but I didn't want to spoil things.

'We'd better hurry then, if you want to catch Kristof,' said Lizzie, walking off. 'There's been a change of plan. They're moving the prisoners out this afternoon.'

Chapter 26

Lizzie and Phil didn't know why the plan had been changed.

The officer in charge of the camp had turned up in the kitchen that morning and had told Mr Morgan that the orders had come to move the prisoners that day.

'Well, keep this under your hat,' said Lizzie, and she began to whisper. '*I think there's a ship sailing from Liverpool tomorrow, so they want them on that.* Now . . .' she said, speaking normal again, 'what's this grand idea of yours, Al?'

So Aldo told them. Freddo chipped in once or twice, keeping an eye on me just to make sure I wasn't going to make fun, or anything. We were up by the top field now, on the last stretch of the lane leading down to the farm.

Lizzie listened and nodded as the boys talked. She looked at Cousin Phil a couple of times, especially when Aldo said how he thought that Kristof would be able to find Mr Moretti in one of the Australian camps and deliver his letter.

Cousin Phil looked away and started whistling some tune.

Billy and Vic walked along, mouths open. They didn't say a word. I think it was hard for them to take it all in.

'What if the ship isn't going to Australia, Al?' said Lizzie, very gently. 'That would put a bit of a damper on things, wouldn't it?'

'It will be going there, though,' said Aldo, sure as anything.

Freddo looked at Lizzie. 'It's worth a try, innit?' he said. His eyes were wanting her to say yes, for his brother's sake.

Lizzie looked right back at him. 'It is,' she said. 'Come on. We'd better get a move on and deliver that letter to Kristof.'

We hurried on down the lane, chatting, going over what had happened with Ivor and his gang.

Aldo laughed. 'He ran away,' he said. 'He didn't know we had a secret weapon.' He patted Captain on the head. The dog wagged his tail and licked Aldo's hand.

'Hang on,' said Cousin Phil all of a sudden in that loud voice of hers.

Billy and Vic jumped a bit.

'It's all gone a bit quiet down there, hasn't it?' She was pointing at the big house.

She was right. Even from where we were standing, the place looked deserted and when we hurried on down the lane to get a closer look, we could see that it was. No soldiers around, no army lorries, no prisoners.

'Perhaps they're all at the farm,' said Lizzie. 'Come on. Let's run.'

But the farmyard was empty too, apart from the usual chickens clucking around.

No prisoners here, either.

Freddo and me looked at Aldo. He had taken the crumpled envelope out of his pocket ready to give to Kristof, but there was no Kristof.

Aldo said, a bit anxious, 'Perhaps they're working somewhere else on the farm.'

Lizzie marched into the farmhouse. 'Daddy,' she called. 'We're back. What's going on?'

Cousin Phil headed for the pig shed. 'Uncle Gwynfor,' she yelled. 'Are you in there?'

Billy and Vic looked around, liking what they saw. 'It's good, this place,' said Billy. 'No wonder you wanted to keep it to yourself.'

There were voices in the house. Mr Morgan came to the front door. 'Hello, boys,' he said. 'Lizzie tells me you've been in a bit of a fight. Who won?'

'We did,' said Freddo.

'With a bit of help,' I said.

'Well done,' said Mr Morgan. Then he looked at Billy and Vic. 'Found some orphans on the way, did you?'

He laughed, but Billy and Vic just stared at him. 'Don't worry,' he told them. 'You'll get used to us.'

'Where's Kristof?' Aldo asked. 'Where's he working?'

'He's gone, Al,' said Mr Morgan.

Aldo gave such a big gasp that Mr Morgan laughed again. Lizzie nudged him to stop.

'They've all gone,' he said. 'You missed them by about . . . oh . . . six or seven minutes.'

'That's Ivor Ingrams's fault,' said Freddo, angrily. 'If he hadn't stopped us, we'd have been here in time.'

Aldo grew tearful. 'Where've they gone?'

'They've taken them down to Berw Junction,' said Mr Morgan in a whisper that everyone could hear. 'Putting them on the afternoon train to Crewe, I believe. For a connection to Liverpool.' He winked at us. 'Top Secret, that is, mind. Hush-hush!'

169

'What's Top Secret?' Cousin Phil came back into the yard.

'The prisoners have gone,' said Aldo. He wiped his eyes, but I could see they were a bit teary.

'Aw, well, you gave it a good try,' said Cousin Phil, but that made him even worse. He sat down on the bench by the side of the front door. His head dropped onto his chest.

The rest of us looked at him, a bit uncomfortable. Freddo went to sit with him. He put his arm round Aldo's big shoulders. He was trying to make Aldo feel better, but all it did was to start him off crying properly.

'So what's all this about then?' asked Mr Morgan.

Lizzie explained while her father stood in the doorway, looking down on Aldo, all sad on the bench.

Mr Morgan listened very seriously. He didn't say anything about it being a daft idea. 'You know, you boys could still get to Berw before the train goes.'

'How?' asked Lizzie. 'If the lorry left seven minutes ago, they'll never get there in time.'

'Not by road, they won't,' said Mr Morgan. 'But they could take the short cut. You could show them, Lizzie.'

Chapter 27

Where we lived, the main roads usually ran along the bottom of the valleys.

So, if you wanted to drive to a place over the hill, you usually had to follow the road to the end of your valley and then double back up the next one.

Sometimes there were roads that did go up and over the hillsides, but not near Tŷ Cornant. There were paths, though, old tracks that cut over the top of the hill and down the other side. That's what Mr Morgan was suggesting. 'If you take the path through Garth Wood, you might just do it, Liz. You got half an hour.'

Aldo lifted his head up from his chest a bit. He sniffed and wiped his dribbly nose.

But Lizzie said, 'It's too far, Daddy. We won't make it in time.'

Mr Morgan raised his eyebrows and gave a little nod of his head towards Aldo sitting on the bench. '*For his sake*,' he seemed to be saying.

'Give it a go,' he said to Lizzie. Then, to us, 'You're all good runners, in't you, boys?'

'Oh yes,' we all said.

Aldo shot up off the bench. 'You bet!'

'Right then,' said Mr Morgan. 'Better get going. You know the way, don't you, Lizzie?'

'Of course,' she said. 'You boys start off up the hill. I'll catch you up. There's something I need to get.'

171

She turned to go into the farmhouse, then stopped and said, 'Give me a hand, Rob, will you?' Her look meant she wasn't going to take no for an answer.

'Yes,' I said and, as I followed her indoors, I saw my friends race out of the yard, like greyhounds from a trap.

'Good luck, boys!' Mr Morgan shouted. 'Run like the wind! Get that letter to Australia!'

It was dark in the kitchen after the daylight outside. Lizzie was on her knees, searching around in a cupboard. 'I'm surprised at you,' she said.

'Why?'

'For going along with Aldo's plan. It's a bit mad, isn't it?'

'Dunno . . . maybe . . .' Her questions made me want to stick up for my friend, no matter what I really felt about the idea.

Lizzie found what she was looking for. An old rucksack it was, with something inside. She stood up. She hadn't needed my help. She just wanted to find out what I was thinking. 'You don't believe the letter will ever get to Australia, do you?' she said.

'No. But Aldo hopes it will.'

Lizzie nodded. 'Hope's good. Keeps people going.'

'Yes,' I said. 'So that's why I'll help him get it to Kristof.'

'Fair dos,' said Lizzie, strapping the rucksack to her back. 'That's enough of a reason for me.' She made for the door.

'You're a good friend, Robert,' she said. Then she was out into the yard, me following.

Captain started to pad along with us, but Cousin Phil

said, 'Stop! Lie down.' So he dropped to the floor and gave a little whine as he saw us go.

'You better stay and help me, Phil,' said Mr Morgan.

'I was hoping you'd say that,' she laughed, and she waved us off and bellowed, 'Good luck!'

Lizzie was a good runner. By the time we caught up with the others at the top of the lane, I was panting like a steam train. Without anyone saying, we all stopped for a bit of a breather.

Aldo's face was bright red. He was a bit too heavy to do much running, but he wasn't complaining. He just wanted to get his letter to Kristof, so that's what kept him going.

'Right, boys,' said Lizzie after what seemed like only a few seconds. 'That's enough. No time for sunbathing.'

It was downhill from then on, so it was all a bit easier. We strung out in a line behind Lizzie like a pack of animals following the leader. Aldo was the last, so every now and then, Freddo would drop back to see he was all right. 'I am, Fred,' he'd puff. 'I am.'

We whooped and hollered across the grass and gorse, jumping the molehills and splashing through the boggy bits. Very soon, the next valley came into view. Like all our valleys, there were long lines of houses strung out along the sides. There was a river and, in the distance, one of the pits.

'And there's Berw Junction,' said Lizzie, stopping and pointing. It was straight below us. You could almost make out the platforms. You could definitely see where all the different sets of tracks linked up to make it a busy station.

'Come on,' she said. 'It looks near enough but it's a bit of a way still.' Then she was off again, taking long strides to get her down the hillside to where a line of trees marked the start of Garth Wood. We galloped after her.

It was cool in the forest. The pine trees cut out most of the sun. The ground was springier in there too. The path was bouncy with pine needles. 'Wait for us, Lizzie,' we yelled as she zoomed ahead, dodging under the low branches.

'Come on, slowcoaches,' she laughed. But after a while she did wait and we did get a bit of a breather, before we were off again.

The forest seemed to go on for ages. I didn't know how we were doing for time, and I couldn't see how far down the hillside we'd come, either. So it was a bit of a shock when we finally got clear of the trees and saw that we didn't have that far to go. We stopped again to get our breath back.

'There they are, look,' Freddo pointed. 'There's the lorry.'

We were near enough now to see it pulling up in the station yard. The lorry had a canvas roof on, so people wouldn't see the prisoners, I suppose.

At the same time, a train whistle blew from somewhere down the valley.

'Is that their train?' Aldo gasped, a bit panicky.

'I don't know,' said Lizzie. 'But it's no good standing here to find out, is it?'

She took a few steps on the path that had brought us out of the wood. It looked like it wound on down the hillside in zigzags. 'That's going to take us too long,' said Lizzie, almost to herself. 'We'll have to go straight down.'

'It's all stony,' Billy said. 'We'll fall.'

'We'll go on our bottoms then,' said Lizzie. 'Follow me.'

She tucked the legs of her dungarees into her socks and, half standing, half crouching, she plunged feet first into the loose stones that covered this bit of the hillside.

'Come on!' she called back. 'Don't think about it.'

She was almost sliding down now, on her bottom, using her hands to balance.

With a big 'YOWWWWWW' Vic took the plunge, then Freddo, then me. Little rivers of stones tumbled around us as we went slipping and sliding down the hill. Behind me, I could hear Billy and Freddo and Aldo joining in. An extra big river of stones came rolling past when Aldo started off.

I grazed my hands and bruised my back but I didn't care. Nor did anyone else, I think. We were all yelling and laughing, and very, very excited now we knew we were nearly there.

We tumbled into a heap at the bottom, still laughing, but Lizzie was on her feet, dusting herself down, ready to move on. We were at the top of a *gwli* leading through the houses.

'Come on, boys,' she said. 'Not far now. It's just along that street down there.'

We set off down the *gwli*, turned a corner, and saw the station straight ahead.

'Fred,' Aldo called out. 'What if the soldiers . . . don't let us . . . ?' He was panting hard, struggling to keep up. '. . . What if they don't let us . . . get close to Kristof?'

175

Freddo turned round and ran backwards. 'Don't worry, Al. We'll think of something.'

'I already have,' yelled Lizzie.

Then another train whistle came echoing up the valley.

Chapter 28

'Stand back on platform 3. Train approaching.'

That's what we heard the porter shout out as we skidded into the station yard.

The army lorry was there, but there was no one in it.

'Are we too late?' Aldo puffed. Our run had taken it out of him. His face was red. He was sweating and he was getting very anxious.

'No. The train's not here yet,' said Freddo.

'Platform 3, quick,' said Lizzie.

Berw Junction had a lot of platforms. To get to platform 3, you had to go down some stone stairs and through a tunnel under the tracks.

We took the steps two at a time. Lizzie led the way. The sound of our footsteps bounced off the walls of the tunnel.

'It don't half stink in here,' Billy said, holding his nose.

'Wee,' grunted Vic.

'Come on, Al,' Freddo panted. 'Nearly there.'

A whistle sounded again, closer now.

'Stand back. Train arriving.' The porter's voice echoed through the tunnel.

We leapt up the stairs. Lizzie was already at the top. 'There they are,' she said, as the rest of us spilled onto the platform. The prisoners were at the far end, away from the other people waiting for the train. They were huddled in a little group. Each one of them had a small brown cardboard suitcase. The soldiers were standing in a little circle around them, rifles at the ready in case of trouble.

We could hear the train getting closer, chugging up the line. It would be here any minute.

'There's Kristof,' Aldo shouted. His face broke into a smile.

Along the platform, Kristof must have heard him because he swung round to look at us.

The guards heard too. They all turned and looked. One of them raised his rifle a bit higher.

'Oh no,' said Freddo. 'It's the soldier who sent us away when we got the puppet back. He's not going to let us get near, for definite.'

Lizzie took the rucksack off her back and reached inside. She said, 'Give me the letter, Al. I'll take it to him.'

'They won't let you give it him either,' I said. 'They'll think it's a secret message or something.'

'I know,' said Lizzie. 'But I'm going to give him this too. I'll fold the letter up with it.'

From her rucksack, she took out the little wooden rocking horse. The one Kristof had made when he'd got pally with Aldo. 'I'll tell them he left it behind,' she said.

Aldo gripped the letter tight in his hand. 'I want to give it him myself.' He had a stubborn look.

'Lizzie's right, Al,' said Freddo. 'They're not going to let you get close.'

'Stand back!' the porter shouted. 'Train arriving.'

The engine came thundering up the track. It made a clattering noise as it crossed over the points just outside the station. Big clouds of grey smoke shot up from its chimney.

Me and Billy and Vic turned to watch it.

'Give her the letter, Al,' Freddo begged. 'Please.'

Lizzie joined in. 'It's the only way we'll get it to him, Al. Honest.'

The engine came rumbling into the station. Smoke clouds swirled around us. The brakes squealed.

'Al,' Freddo shouted above the din. 'If you want the letter to find its way to Papa . . . give it to Lizzie now.'

That did it. With a little moan, Aldo handed over his precious letter. Lizzie grabbed it and stuffed it into the pocket on the front of her dungarees and went tearing off along the platform. She had to dodge past people and mail carts and cases, but she kept pace with the engine as it trundled into the platform. She made it to the group of prisoners just as the train came to a stop with a great loud *HISSSSSSS*!

Some of the soldiers turned to watch her arrive. The others shuffled the prisoners to the edge of the platform ready to get on the train.

We saw Lizzie talking to the soldiers. She pointed at Kristof. He looked at Lizzie and then at us.

The train doors were being opened and people were getting off.

The soldiers edged the prisoners forward.

Lizzie was showing the rocking horse to the two soldiers who had sent us packing.

People were starting to get on the train.

Some of the prisoners did too, with their guards.

'It's not going to work,' said Aldo, disappointed.

'Everyone on board now!' the porter shouted. 'This train is ready to leave.'

Kristof was nudged forward by one of the guards. They still wouldn't let Lizzie get near him.

She looked back at us and made a face as if to say, 'It's not working.'

'We'll have to do something. Quick!' said Freddo, very panicky. 'Grab their attention.'

At the top of the stairs to the platform, just where we were standing, was a pile of silvery metal milk churns. Like big shiny dustbins, with lids. They were used to take the milk from the farms to the towns round about.

All of a sudden, Aldo bent down and picked one up. They were empty at that time of day, but they were still heavy.

'Al, mind, mun,' said Freddo. 'You'll hurt yourself.'

But Aldo didn't care.

The train guard blew his whistle.

The last few prisoners were being hurried into the carriage.

Aldo lifted the shiny metal churn high above his head. He gave a great yodelling yell, like Tarzan of the Apes.

The few people making their way towards the stairs moved back.

The soldiers stopped and turned.

And Aldo dropped the heavy churn with a mighty CLANG! The big round metal lid sprang loose and rolled down the platform.

The soldiers edged along to see what the trouble was. For a moment, they took their eyes off the prisoners.

And Lizzie reached into her dungaree pocket and handed the letter to Kristof.

'What the heck are you doing, you boys?' The porter

came running up the platform. He had to jump over the lid of the churn as it bowled along.

'Sorry, mister. It was an accident,' Freddo shouted. We all got ready to run though.

The guard's whistle blew again. Train doors slammed shut. The soldiers turned back to the prisoners and pushed the last stragglers on board. Then they jumped on too and closed the door behind them.

The porter was halfway down the platform now, chasing the rolling lid.

The train hooter sounded and, smoke pouring from the chimney, the engine started to chug its way out of the station.

'She did it, Al,' I said. 'Did you see? Lizzie gave the letter to Kristof.'

'I did see,' he said. He had a great big smile on his face. 'I did!'

Lizzie came marching back along the platform. She was trying not to grin, but you could tell she was pleased with what she'd done. She had the little rocking horse in her hand.

'Look!' said Billy, all of a sudden. He pointed at the carriages, just about to round the curve that led away from the station.

There was a man waving from one of the windows.

It was Kristof. He was holding on tight to something in his hand. He gave a big nod. Big enough for us all to see.

'Oh,' said Aldo. 'My letter's on its way to Papa.'

Then the porter came towards us, face like thunder, so we scarpered.

Chapter 29

We raced up the steps from the tunnel under the tracks and into the station yard. We were full of ourselves, happy as sand boys that the plan had worked. Just!

'You frightened me out of my wits, Al,' Billy grinned, 'when you gave that yell.'

'Haven't heard you do that for ages, Al,' said Freddo. 'You used to do that up the Pandy.'

'Tarzan to the rescue, eh?' said Lizzie. 'Well done, strong man!'

Aldo beamed – and blushed. 'Well, someone had to help you, Lizzie,' he said and pointed at us. 'They wasn't doing nothing.'

'Oh, thanks a lot, Al,' said Freddo. 'We only got you here, that's all. Anyway, it's Lizzie we ought to thank.'

We dawdled across the station yard. The porter had given us a right telling-off for doing something so dangerous, but he hadn't followed us, so we could take our time.

'Thank you, Lizzie,' said Aldo and he made as if to give her a big hug.

'Dodge, Lizzie,' Freddo shouted. 'If you don't want your ribs cracked.'

She laughed, but she dodged out of the way all the same.

Now all we had to do was slog back up the hillside over to Tŷ Cornant. I don't think any of us was looking forward to that.

The driver of the army lorry came up the steps from

the tunnel. He was by himself because the other soldiers had got on the train with the prisoners.

'Oh, oh,' he said when he saw Aldo. 'It's young Tarzan.' Then he laughed. 'And the apes!'

'Ha ha,' we said. 'Very funny.'

Then Lizzie asked, 'You going back to Tŷ Cornant?'

'I am,' he said. 'In a bit.' He opened the driver's door and swung himself up in the cab.

'Give us a lift, then.'

'Can't do that,' the soldier said. 'I'm on duty.'

'But the prisoners have all gone,' said Lizzie. 'There's no one around to see you.'

The driver looked down at us, thinking.

'It's a long way, mister,' said Billy.

'Uphill,' said Freddo.

'And I think there's some of my cousin's honey cake left over,' said Lizzie, edging nearer the lorry.

The driver laughed. 'How could I refuse?' he said. 'But I'm not going yet, mind. I've got to wait for the next train to pick up a couple of lads.'

'That's all right,' said Freddo. 'We're not in any hurry. Not now.'

So we sat down on the low wall outside the station and waited for the train to come. It was supposed to arrive in five minutes, the soldier said. There were a couple of men on it who were going to be the first of the new guards up at Tŷ Cornant.

'You expecting more prisoners then?' Lizzie asked.

'Oh, aye,' said the soldier. 'We're picking up a lot of those Luftwaffe boys now. Have to start building bigger camps soon.'

'Or send them all to the Dominions,' said Aldo.

'Aye, that's right,' the soldier said, and settled back in the driving seat. He pulled his army cap down over his eyes. Up the valley, a train whistle hooted. 'That'll be it,' he said, but he didn't move.

We didn't either. We were happy to sit there in the sunshine, keeping one eye out in case the porter turned up. 'It was a good idea of yours to bring that rocking horse,' said Freddo to Lizzie.

She smiled. 'Well, I thought we'd need some excuse to get near Kristof. And there was a better chance of me doing that than any of you.'

'Clever!'

'Mmm,' said Lizzie. 'Nearly didn't work out though, did it?'

'No,' Vic agreed.

'But good old Aldo saved the day,' said Lizzie.

Vic nodded. 'He did.'

Aldo grinned and beat his chest, just like Tarzan in the pictures.

It was good to see him happy again.

Nobody said anything after that. We sat there, just thinking our own thoughts. I had found things out that I didn't know before, some not very nice things. About myself, I mean. I discovered that sometimes I could get very jealous. Stupid, really, when it came to Freddo and Aldo. If you're true friends, really true friends, that's the way you'll stay. No matter what.

Billy edged close up to Lizzie and whispered, 'Do you think the letter will ever get to Australia?'

'Robert doesn't, do you, Robert?' said Lizzie quietly, squinting sideways at me with a bit of a smile.

'No,' I said, looking at Freddo and Al. I wasn't sure if they'd heard and if they did, how they'd react. 'I do think it was a bit of a daft idea.' Then to lighten things up a bit, I went on, 'But Aldo thinks it'll get there. So that's the main thing.'

'I do,' said Aldo. He'd heard all right.

Then we went quiet again, looking at the people coming and going. Some were carrying cases and bags. One man had a live chicken under his arm. It squawked a lot and made us laugh. On the platform, we could hear the porter shouting out: 'Next Cardiff train on platform 4. Stand back from the platform edge.'

'And watch out for the milk churns!' Billy said in an announcer kind of voice. That made us all laugh some more.

The soldier sat up in his seat and pushed his cap out of his eyes. 'Right, you lot. Listen.' He opened the door and jumped down onto the road. 'I'm putting you in the back, out of sight,' he said. 'So, no messing.'

'Fair enough,' said Aldo. 'We'll be quiet as mice. Honest.'

'You better be, Tarzan,' the soldier said. 'I'm not supposed to be doing this, so if there's any trouble I'll turf you all out and you'll have to walk it. OK?'

'OK,' we said.

The soldier walked to the back of the lorry and lifted up the bottom of the canvas cover. 'Hop in,' he said.

Billy and Vic got in first, then Lizzie and me scrambled

up, then Freddo. He leaned out to give Aldo a hand, but Lizzie had to help him. The soldier gave a final push, too. Aldo ended up on his stomach, on the wooden floor of the lorry, gasping a bit like a landed fish. 'Thanks,' he puffed, and crawled forward to sit with his back to the driver's cab.

It wasn't dark in the back of the lorry, because light came through the greeny-brown canvas cover. It was hot and stuffy though, so Billy and Vic edged to one side and lifted the cover, just enough to poke their heads out and get some air.

'What you doing?' the soldier shouted. 'I said no messing, didn't I?'

'It's hot in here, mister,' Billy said.

'Like an oven,' Vic added.

'Well, when the train arrives, you'll have to stick your heads back in again,' the soldier said.

'Aye, we will!'

The train was getting nearer. We could hear it steaming along the valley.

Aldo and Freddo poked their heads out of the canvas.

I was going to, but Lizzie said, very quiet, 'I bet you're happy now, aren't you, Robert?' I knew what she meant, but she said it anyway. 'Now Kristof's gone?'

'Yes.'

I wanted to change the subject. I sat up and lifted the canvas.

The train came thundering into the station. A few last stragglers came running along the station yard and scooted into the tunnel under the tracks.

The porter shouted, 'Cardiff train. Cardiff train.'

'Right, heads in,' the soldier said. 'And play dead till I let you out.'

He walked round the lorry, pulling down the edge of the cover. He gave it a few pats to straighten it out.

'Ouch,' said Vic, who was a bit slow pulling his head in and got clobbered.

Then we all lay down on the floor of the lorry and listened to the comings and goings outside.

People came out of the station, chatting and laughing. A car drove into the yard to pick someone up.

Train doors slammed shut. Then we heard the driver call out: 'You the lads from Brecon barracks?'

Voices shouted back. They were.

'Hop in up front,' said the soldier. 'I'll put your kit in the truck.' We heard him jump down, and, next thing, the canvas was lifted up at the back of the lorry and two heavy kitbags were thrown in, just missing us.

'Blinking heck,' whispered Freddo. 'It's like dodging a bloomin' Stuka.'

Aldo giggled. Well, sort of snuffled really because he was trying not to be heard and Freddo had put his hand over his mouth anyway.

The driver got back in his cab, closed the door and started the engine. It was loud and rattly, but we started to roll out of the station yard.

Then we heard a man's voice shouting, but over the roar of the engine we couldn't hear it very clearly or make out what he was saying.

The lorry came to a stop and the driver switched off the engine. We heard him say, 'What's that, butt?'

The man came nearer.

'You going anywhere near Tregwyn?' he said.

And my heart did a flip flop!

I knew that voice. I swear I did. I sat up.

Freddo did too. He'd heard it. He knew who it was.

'Give us a lift, butt,' the man was saying. 'I'm bushed, aye.'

I wanted to lift the canvas, but I didn't dare. Not because I was scared of the driver, but because I didn't want to find out I was wrong.

'I been away,' the man was saying, and then I couldn't wait any longer.

I rolled up the canvas as high as I could and shoved my head out.

The driver shouted, 'I said no messing!' He banged on the back of the cab.

The man was standing near the lorry.

Yes! Oh, yes!

It was who I thought it was. Who I hoped it would be.

He was wearing a dark-blue navy uniform and he had a kitbag over his shoulder. He seemed a bit dirty and a bit tired and a bit thin. And when he saw my head pop out of the canvas, he looked as amazed as I was.

'Robert?' he said, not believing. 'Rob?'

He dropped the bag and moved towards the lorry.

I thought he was limping a bit, but he was laughing too. He opened his arms wide. 'What you doing here?'

I jumped out of the lorry and ran to meet him. 'What YOU doing here?' I yelled.

Then my dad lifted me up in a great big hug and I couldn't say any more.

Chapter 30

Cheers and yells came spilling out of the lorry, and five heads poked out from under the canvas.

'*Duw, Duw*,' my dad said, putting me down at last. 'I didn't know you were laying on a welcome committee, Rob.'

Then he limped over to Aldo and Freddo and ruffled their hair. 'Good to see you, boys,' he said. 'How's your mam and dad?'

'Tell you later, Mr Prosser,' Freddo chipped in quick before Aldo could say anything.

'Right you are,' said my dad. Then he said, 'Ow-be, boys?' to Billy and Vic, and, 'Who's this then?' to Lizzie.

'I'm Lizzie Morgan,' she said, holding her hand out to shake Dad's. 'I'm their friend.'

He wiped his hand on his trousers and shook her hand back. 'Nice to meet you.'

The driver came round the side of the lorry. 'Sorry to break up your little party,' he said. 'But I gotta be going.'

'Can you drop us at Tregwyn then, butt?' asked my dad.

'Aye. S'pose so,' said the driver. 'Hop in the back.'

Then he went round to his driver's cab. We heard him muttering, 'Knew I shouldn't have given this bunch a lift.' He swung up into his seat and told the soldiers sitting with him: 'Knew they'd be trouble.' But he was laughing when he said it. They laughed too.

My dad picked up his kitbag and climbed up, a bit slowly, into the back of the lorry. The engine coughed into life and we pulled out of the station yard.

We rolled the canvas roof right up but the driver didn't seem to mind.

As we rumbled along, in the evening sunlight, my dad sat and told us what had happened to him.

He'd been put on a ship called the *Hero*. 'A destroyer,' he said. When they'd finished fighting in Norway, they'd sailed to the Mediterranean Sea. He'd been in a battle near an island called Crete.

'That's not the Dominions,' Aldo said, out of the blue.

My dad looked at him a bit puzzled, but Freddo said, 'Don't worry, Mr Prosser. Go on.'

It turned out that my dad had been wounded in the battle. Shot in the leg. 'Nothing serious,' he said. 'It'll mend in no time. And, anyway, it got me some leave, didn't it?'

That's why he was here. They'd sent him home for a few weeks to get better.

'Why didn't you write and tell us, Dad?'

'I did, mun. I wrote lots of letters.'

'We did too,' I told him.

He shook his head. 'None of them got through. But that's what happens in wartime.'

Aldo leaned across and said, very serious, 'Maybe, if you could have given a letter to someone . . . to deliver it in person, like . . . it would have got through.'

My dad looked at him a bit more puzzled, but all he said was, 'Aye, you might be right there, boy.'

Sounds of singing came from the driver's cab.

'Someone's happy,' said Lizzie, meaning the driver. But she could have been talking about me.

My heart felt fit to burst. My dad had been wounded, but he was still alive. That was the most important thing. So nothing could spoil my happiness now. Not even the nagging little thought that Ivor and his butties would want to get even, sometime.

Never mind. None of that mattered because today was special. Today was the day my dad came back from the war. For a bit, anyway.

Billy piped up: 'I know this one . . .' He'd been listening to the driver and the soldiers. They'd moved on to another song and were singing it at the tops of their voices.

'What is it?' asked Vic.

'It's from that film with the puppet,' Billy said. 'The one Aldo had.'

'*Pinocchio*,' I said.

'It's that song about wishing on a star,' said Lizzie. 'And making your dreams come true.'

'I'll go along with that,' said Dad. 'I've been wishing for this day a long time.'

He gave me a big smile and joined in the singing.

Lizzie started up and so did Vic, then Billy and Freddo and Al. And then me.

Rowdy as anything, we were all singing at the tops of our voices as the lorry rattled its way home.

About the Author

Alan Lambert grew up in the Merthyr Valley but now lives in London. He is a former teacher and has also worked for the BBC as Commissioning Executive for primary-school programmes.

The rough treatment experienced by some of the Italian families living and working in the Valleys during the Second World War inspired Alan to write his original story *Roberto's War*. The themes of friendship and growing up in a close community are present in both novels, as well as a strong sense of history.